Eyes On You

Also By Laura Kaye

Eyes On You

A BLASPHEMY NOVELLA

By Laura Kaye

1001 Dark Nights

EVIL EYE
CONCEPTS

Eyes On You
A Blasphemy Novella
By Laura Kaye

1001 Dark Nights
Copyright 2017 Laura Kaye
ISBN: 978-1-945920-19-6

Foreword: Copyright 2014 M. J. Rose
Published by Evil Eye Concepts, Incorporated

Acknowledgments from the Author

Some books take you by surprise, and *Eyes on You* was definitely one. Of necessity, it came out in a rush of words, but I couldn't have slowed it down if I tried. Wolf and Liv just leapt onto the page, surprising and exciting me and making me laugh (and sometimes blush). And I have Liz Berry to thank for the opportunity to make that happen. 1001 Dark Nights is such an amazing and special project to be a part of, and I'm honored that I get to share stories I love through it. Thanks Liz and Jillian Stein for all you do to support and encourage and be there for me – it means the world.

Thanks also to KP Simmon who was there every step of the way, taking the heat off so I could focus on those fast and furious words. And thanks to my amazing critique partner, Christi Barth, for reading right behind me and making me shine as you always do. I appreciate having such amazingly supportive women in my life.

Thanks also to my Heroes and my Reader Girls, who give me motivation and encouragement even when they don't know they're doing it. And thanks, as always, to my readers, who take my characters in to their hearts and allow me to tell their stories again and again. ~LK

Sign up for the 1001 Dark Nights Newsletter
and be entered to win a Tiffany Key necklace.

There's a contest every month!

Go to www.1001DarkNights.com to subscribe.

As a bonus, all subscribers will receive a free
1001 Dark Nights story
The First Night
by Lexi Blake & M.J. Rose

One Thousand and One Dark Nights

Once upon a time, in the future...

*I was a student fascinated with stories and learning.
I studied philosophy, poetry, history, the occult, and
the art and science of love and magic. I had a vast
library at my father's home and collected thousands
of volumes of fantastic tales.*

*I learned all about ancient races and bygone
times. About myths and legends and dreams of all
people through the millennium. And the more I read
the stronger my imagination grew until I discovered
that I was able to travel into the stories... to actually
become part of them.*

*I wish I could say that I listened to my teacher
and respected my gift, as I ought to have. If I had, I
would not be telling you this tale now.
But I was foolhardy and confused, showing off
with bravery.*

*One afternoon, curious about the myth of the
Arabian Nights, I traveled back to ancient Persia to
see for myself if it was true that every day Shahryar
(Persian: شهريار, "king") married a new virgin, and then
sent yesterday's wife to be beheaded. It was written
and I had read, that by the time he met Scheherazade,
the vizier's daughter, he'd killed one thousand
women.*

Something went wrong with my efforts. I arrived in the midst of the story and somehow exchanged places with Scheherazade — a phenomena that had never occurred before and that still to this day, I cannot explain.

Now I am trapped in that ancient past. I have taken on Scheherazade's life and the only way I can protect myself and stay alive is to do what she did to protect herself and stay alive.

Every night the King calls for me and listens as I spin tales. And when the evening ends and dawn breaks, I stop at a point that leaves him breathless and yearning for more. And so the King spares my life for one more day, so that he might hear the rest of my dark tale.

As soon as I finish a story... I begin a new one... like the one that you, dear reader, have before you now.

To everyone searching for that feeling of being deeply and intensely alive, listen closely to yourself, for no one knows you better.

"There is a voice inside which speaks and says, *'This is the real me!'*"
~ William James, American psychologist and philosopher

Chapter 1

Things that would be better than being on this date, Liv Foster thought as she stared across the high-boy bar table at her so-called perfect match, Jerry. *A popcorn kernel stuck between my teeth...finding a snake in my car...a pelvic exam...* She took a sip of her Prosecco, hoping the bubbles would make her feel better as the guy continued to complain about the hour-long wait for a table.

"...This really is unacceptable. I mean, it's not even that busy in here," he said, running his hand over his short black hair. He was attractive enough, although it was clear that the picture on his online dating profile was at least ten years old. Maybe more. She'd thought they were a few years apart in age, but she suspected it was more like ten or fifteen. "I just hate incompetence, don't you?"

Liv eyeballed the guy. You know, the one who hadn't bothered to make a reservation at a swanky new restaurant located in a hotel just two blocks from the baseball stadium on a Friday night before a Baltimore Orioles game. It took everything she had not to roll her eyes. "Yeah, I really do."

He huffed out a breath and shook his head, then started stretching and turning in his seat like he was looking for their waitress. In the thirty minutes they'd already waited, the two of them had apparently exhausted every small talk conversation of which he was capable. Jobs—she was a florist and he was an architect. The weather—sure had been a hot summer! Siblings—neither had any, so that was a short topic. Prior relationships—Liv hadn't offered any gory details—though she had them in spades, whereas she almost felt like she knew Jerry's ex, Angela, personally.

"So, what are you going to order?" Jerry asked.

Liv tilted her head. "Uh, well, I don't know yet. I haven't seen their menu."

He pulled a face. "I don't use menus."

"You…what? How does that work?" she asked with a little laugh. Was he joking? She honestly couldn't tell.

He shrugged. "I don't use menus."

In her mind's eye, she pictured her childhood golden retriever, Howie, tilting his head. Then tilting it even more. She was seriously channeling some Howie just then. "But…how do you know what you want to order?"

He waved a hand around at the restaurant as if it were self-evident. "It's a steakhouse. They have steak."

"Oh. Uh. Right." The waitress's appearance saved Liv from trying to come up with a better response. Right in that moment, she thought she *almost* would've given anything to turn back time to when she and Caleb were still happy. When they were looking forward to their wedding, their honeymoon, and their life together beyond all the celebrations. But she was beyond wishing for something that could never be—especially when she deserved so much better. Besides, too much of what she'd thought she'd had with Caleb hadn't been real, had it? And she never wanted to go back to that. Not ever again.

But, man. Jerry. Jerry was too freaking real. And Liv was still deserving better. But she was stuck on this ride at least until she'd choked down the last bite of her steak.

"Can I get you another round of drinks?" their waitress asked.

"Can we just eat here in the bar?" Jerry asked. "This wait is ridiculous."

"Oh, sure. Of course," the young woman said, pasting on a smile. Working in customer service, Liv knew what it took to deal with assholes like Jerry. And being three years single and back on the dating market, she was starting to know what it was like to date them, too. "I'll grab you menus."

He put a hand on the woman's arm. "That won't be necessary. We don't need menus. I'll just order for us."

Liv wondered if her expression appeared as stunned as the waitress's, especially when the woman stepped out of Jerry's grasp and looked at Liv as if to ask if this was okay.

No. Definitely, totally not okay. "Actually," Liv said, trying to keep her irritation in check. Because dang if breaking that *be nice* habit wasn't hard as heck. "I—"

"I'll have the ten-ounce Kobe filet mignon and she'll have the six-ounce Kobe filet. Both medium well with loaded baked potatoes and asparagus." He stared at the waitress.

The waitress shook her head. "I'm sorry, sir, we don't have Kobe beef. We have an excellent local provider of American beef, and we have Wagyu."

"That's okay," Liv said. "I prefer ribeye anyway. Medium *rare*."

"Ribeye is too fatty," Jerry said, looking at her like she was a child who'd disappointed him before his gaze returned to the hapless woman standing beside their table. "And I'd like to speak to your manager. Because what kind of steakhouse doesn't have Kobe beef?"

"I'll get her for you right away," the woman said, nearly running from them. Liv couldn't blame her.

The silence that followed was thick with tension, and Liv almost couldn't decide if she'd hallucinated what'd happened or if this first date was truly just that bad. Jerry wouldn't make eye contact and, instead, peered down at his cell phone beneath the table. So she took the opportunity to survey the diners sitting at the horseshoe-shaped bar near them in the hopes she'd see someone, *anyone*, she knew. *God, please give me a way to escape Mr. I Don't Use Menus.* But God had clearly forsaken her, because the party of three women having a girls' night out were strangers. As were the various groupings of men, some of whom wore Orioles gear and watched the pre-game commentary on the captioned television screens above the bar. An elderly man she didn't know sat alone nearest to their high-boy table nursing a glass of bourbon, and two seats down from him...sat the hottest man Liv had ever seen.

And that was her impression just from seeing him in profile.

He had dark blond hair and a chiseled jaw, and even sitting, it was clear that he was tall. Seriously broad shoulders filled out a dark green button-down shirt, and big hands gripped a glass of water. Now God was just being mean. Because someone was going to get to be with that man tonight while she was stuck here with Jerry of the I Don't Use Menus clan. As she watched, *not*-Jerry pressed his cell phone to his ear and began talking in tones too low for her to hear.

On a sigh, Liv returned her attention to Jerry. Not that it mattered, because his gaze remained fixed on his phone. She drained the rest of her Prosecco and wished someone would bring her the bottle. That wouldn't be too awkward for a first date, right? *Right?*

"How are you folks this evening?" a new woman asked as she stepped to their table. "I'm Ms. Sanderson, the manager."

"Well, Ms. Sanderson, we've been better," Jerry said, launching right into a tirade. "We wanted the Kobe filets."

The manager produced two menus from behind her back like she'd been hiding a present. "I'm happy to recommend some other—"

Jerry blocked the large leather folio from hitting the table. "I don't use menus."

It took Ms. Sanderson a moment to recover, but you could hardly blame her. She glanced at Liv like Liv might impose some sanity on the situation, but the sanity ship seemed to have sailed on this date. "Well, sir, that's really the best way to see what we serve—"

You don't say, Liv thought, pressing her fingers to her lips to smother the smile that threatened.

"Why are you making this so hard?" Jerry asked. "It's a steakhouse. I want your best steak."

"Very good," the manager said with a seemingly sincere smile. "We have several cuts of Wagyu. If you haven't had it before, I highly recommend it."

Red streaks climbed up Jerry's throat and face. "Wagyu is ridiculously expensive, and this is only a first date," he huffed.

"You know what?" Liv said, pushing her chair back before she'd really thought about it. "Whatever you order for me will be fine. I just need to use the restroom."

She'd never run from a restaurant table so fast in her life. Now the question was whether she could run from the restaurant itself. Or, at least, how long she could hide in the bathroom. Or, possibly, whether she ever had to come out at all.

* * * *

Wolf Henrikson watched the sexy stranger flee her table like it was the Titanic and the bathroom was the last available lifeboat. And he couldn't say that he blamed her. He hadn't been trying to eavesdrop on the couple's conversation; it was only that every time the man spoke to anyone from the restaurant's staff, he shouted like he wanted to make the scene he was in fact making.

What the hell was the cute brunette doing with such an asshole anyway? The few times he'd looked around to see if his dinner companion had arrived, he'd noticed the woman sitting not too far away—and she'd made him do a double take every time. Between her glossy chocolate waves, the bright red paint on her bow-tie lips, and the vintage-style red dress with the plunging neckline and the full knee-length skirt, she had the sex appeal of a pinup girl. He couldn't help wondering if she wore garters and thigh-highs beneath that skirt.

Wolf almost regretted that he no longer had any reason to stay at the bar because the scene playing out at the nearby table was like a train wreck he couldn't stop watching. And, oh, he *did* enjoy watching. People were just so fucking interesting, even when they were off their damn rockers.

But the prospective submissive he'd been planning to meet—in public, at her request—had just called to let him know she'd gotten cold feet. He respected the honesty. The BDSM lifestyle wasn't for everyone, and it wasn't something he recommended anyone explore frivolously. But the change in plans left him at loose ends.

Actually, that feeling was a constant presence in his blood these days. Restlessness. Boredom. Dissatisfaction without really being able to pinpoint why.

In anticipation of the meeting, he'd only had water, but he dropped a few dollars on the bar anyway, then pushed off the stool and made for the restrooms at the back. Blasphemy would be hopping soon, and even though he wasn't scheduled to work a shift, he could no doubt find a willing partner to play with there. Though he was one of the twelve Master Dominants and a one-twelfth owner of the city's most exclusive BDSM club, Wolf's particular kink didn't require all the equipment and special rooms that some did. Really, voyeurism and exhibitionism could be enjoyed anywhere. Which was kinda the point.

As long as he could watch, or knew others were watching, or was with someone who got off on being watched, he was all kinds of good.

Or, at least, he used to be. Something had been missing for him in all of it lately, leaving him wondering whether his role in Blasphemy still made the most sense—for him and his partners. A number of the other

Masters had found women to love and to collar, and even to marry. They were committed to the club because it was central to their lives and their relationships. For years, being a part of the scene there had been important to Wolf, giving him a safe place to play and meet likeminded women. But lately, he wasn't getting the same thrill, the same satisfaction out of it. And it left him feeling like a bit of a fraud. Because the Masters of Blasphemy should be all in. The club and its patrons deserved no less.

On a distracted sigh, Wolf stepped into the narrow hallway that led to the restrooms and nearly bowled someone over. "Damn, I'm sorry," he said, grasping the woman's arms to keep from knocking her down. Momentum made it so that he nearly flattened her against the wall, and he got a lungful of a flowery scent from her hair. He prepared for the smackdown his carelessness deserved, but instead what he got was laughter. Full-on, deep belly, throw-your-head-back laughter.

From the sexy pinup girl with the atrocious taste in dinner partners.

"Just...just...an accident," she gasped between bouts of laughter she tried but failed to restrain. "That full body contact with you...will probably end up being the highlight of my night. *Trust me.*"

Wolf grinned as he took in her meaning. He wasn't sure which he appreciated more—her humor, her easy-going nature, or the compliment. Or that dress. Because seeing it up close, *damn*. The V-neckline emphasized the swells of her breasts, and the full, flaring skirt emphasized a narrow waist over satisfyingly full hips.

"That bad?" he asked.

"Oh, mister. The worst. Like, the God's honest worst. And my friend can't rescue me." She rolled her eyes. "So clearly she's fired and I need to hire a new bestie first thing Monday morning."

His grin grew. "From what I overheard, I think you're fully within your rights."

She chuckled. "I didn't even know *not* using menus was a thing. I mean, who does that?"

"Literally no one does that," he said, enjoying her playful manner. She had an interesting face, expressive and a little dramatic. He wondered what she looked like when—

Nope. He couldn't let himself finish that thought. Not unless he wanted her to see exactly how much she appealed to him. And given how her night was going, he doubted that.

"Right? Just my luck. I'm gonna have to cancel my matchmaking service, too. Clearly." She sagged a little against the brick wall, almost like he'd pinned her there. Or commanded her to hold her position. Trying to rein in his lust for her, he dropped his gaze to the floor, but her calves were like artwork perched on a ridiculously sexy pair of strappy black heels with satin ribbon that tied at the ankles.

Wolf's mind exploded with ideas of things he'd do to her—or have her do for him—if they'd come to this place together. If she'd been into the same things he was. If she was his. He licked his lips and shook the thoughts away. He didn't often play with people outside Blasphemy because voyeurism and BDSM were more than most vanilla people could deal with. Admittedly, telling someone that you wanted to fuck them in public where other people could see didn't easily create a good first impression.

"Sounds like your Monday is going to be busy," he managed.

She chuckled. "I think you're right." She heaved a sigh. "Well, thanks for making my night a little better."

He tilted his head and considered, and then the words were out of his mouth before he'd decided if they were a good idea. "I could save you, if you wanted."

"Aw," she said, peering up at him with striking, bright turquoise eyes. "That's the sweetest thing anyone has said to me in a really long damn time. But I guess it would be rude."

"Yeah?" he said, a surprised at how disappointed he was. But her openness and honesty in this short conversation piqued his interest and made him wonder what *else* she might be open to.

"Yeah," she said, also sounding more than a little disappointed.

Which officially intrigued Wolf, because she was interested even if she thought she shouldn't be, given the disastrous date waiting for her. So he held out his hand and threw her a lifeline anyway. Given how he'd been feeling lately, what did he have to lose? "I'm Wolf. I'll be at the bar. Change your mind, just give me a signal."

Her eyes went wide as she slid her hand into his. "Liv. Olivia. And I…don't know what to say."

Wolf leaned down until he could look her eye to eye. Testing her. Observing her. Commanding her. "Say 'thank you, Wolf.'"

When the words finally came, they were a little breathless. "Thank you, Wolf." But she remained pinned to the wall.

Breathing in her floral scent, he waited a moment before he said or did another thing, just to see what she'd do. And all she did was keep her eyes on him. Which was exactly what he'd wanted. Finally, he gave her a wink and then a single nod toward the bar. Only then did she move. With one longing, last glance back, she left the hallway.

And hello, excitement...

Which was the moment Wolf knew he wasn't leaving this restaurant without her.

Chapter 2

It was quite possible that Liv had never been so turned on in her life. She had no idea how she'd peeled herself off that wall, because she wanted nothing more than to stay there. The brightest green eyes she'd ever seen staring at her. Pinning her. Looking like they quite possibly wanted to devour her.

Wolf. It was a crazy name, but holy wow, did it seem to fit. Because something about the way he looked at her made her feel like he was the hunter and she was the prey.

Actually, she was the one who must be crazy. Because *that* feeling should've scared her. Instead, it gave her post-disastrous-date plans that involved her rabbit and her favorite porn scene about a woman who gets taken by a stranger on a subway while everyone around them watches. And there was more than a little likelihood that Liv would be imagining Wolf as the seducer—and her as the seduced—while she watched.

Hating her urge to be nice even when people didn't deserve it, she slid back onto her bar stool and tried to smile at Jerry, but that was hard when he started gloating about how his rudeness had gotten them an offer for free dessert. Liv's hips proved that she could eat the heck out of some dessert, but she'd had her heart set on steak-and-go, so no way did she want to stick around for another course with this guy. At least another glass of Prosecco had been delivered in her absence.

"That's great," she managed, her gaze straying over her date's shoulder to where Wolf was settling onto his bar stool again. He didn't look at her, but somehow she knew that he was aware of her. Keeping tabs on her, even. Would he really rescue her from this date if she gave him a signal? And what would that signal be? Maybe she could wave her white linen napkin like a general surrendering a battle. That thought finally made her smile. The way the bubbly was going to her head helped, too.

Before long, the manager was personally delivering their steaks to the table. The freaking filet mignon, after all. Fine. Whatever.

"Will there be anything else right now?" Ms. Sanderson asked.

"I'll let you know," Jerry said.

Sighing, Liv gave the woman an apologetic smile. "No, thank you." At her wit's end, she finally dropped the niceties. "You know, Jerry, you catch more bees with honey. It's hardly fair to treat a restaurant's staff poorly because they don't serve food they shouldn't be expected to serve because it isn't even on the menu."

He shook his head and shrugged. "You never get what you don't ask for." He pointed his fork at her. "Remember that."

She was still processing his insufferable arrogance when he did something even more astonishing. He reached across the expanse of pressed white linen with his fork and knife...and began cutting her steak.

Liv reared back in her chair, her jaw dropping. "What in the *world* are you doing?"

His gaze rose to meet hers, even while he cut her filet into bite-sized pieces. "I like taking care of little girls," he said, a tendril of heat slipping into his eyes.

Oh, nope. Nopenopenope. A thousand, million times, nope.

She shoved up out of her chair, and the napkin tumbled from her lap to the floor.

As stunned as she was, she wasn't sure which happened first—Jerry asking where she was going or Wolf appearing at her side.

"God, Liv. It really is you," Wolf said. "I worried I'd never see you again."

Liv blinked, swallowed, and played along as she stared up at that handsome Nordic face, all dark-blond and sharp-jawed good looks. "Wolf. Wow. I can't believe it's you."

He stepped closer. "I see you're in the middle of something here..."

"Yes, she is," Jerry said. "If you'll excuse us."

Wolf ignored him. "…but after the way we last parted, I promised myself if I ever saw you again, I wasn't going to let you get away twice."

Liv was nearly breathless. Was he role-playing or talking about their brief encounter? Either way, her response was the same. "I don't want you to let me get away."

She felt out of her element, outside the bounds of propriety, out of control. She had no idea what she was doing here, what she was maybe getting into with this man who was, except for an intense five-minute conversation, a total stranger. She had *no idea*…except that her head said *How could it be worse than my date?* And her instincts said *Go with Wolf, go with Wolf, go with Wolf.* And her body said *And climb him while you're at it.*

"Damn, I hoped you'd say that," Wolf said, green eyes flashing. And then he took her into his arms and kissed her. Right there. In the middle of the bar of a fancy steakhouse. In front of Jerry, who was babbling in outrage that Liv couldn't hear.

Because Wolf dominated every other sense. His hard chest crushing her breasts and his big hands cupping her jaw and sliding into her hair. His cool tongue licking across her lips. His shower-clean scent adding to the Prosecco to make her head swim. Liv stood frozen and still for long seconds, not because she didn't like the kiss, but because she *did*. Oh, man, she really freaking did.

And not just the kiss, though it was by itself the best kiss she'd ever had. It was that Wolf was kissing her where everyone could see him doing it. It was that Jerry's rising volume was drawing even more eyes to them. It was that people were *watching*.

Liv thought about that porn scene she'd been planning to enjoy, and suddenly she felt like she was living it. And she didn't think she'd ever been more turned on in her entire life. Everything tingled as if her nervous system had been plugged in for the very first time. Her nipples puckered so hard they almost ached. Adrenaline had her nearly trembling. And she got wet between her legs. Wet enough that her panties were damp, too.

By the time Wolf released her, she could've fallen to her knees. That was how hard he'd rocked her world. Instead, she just said, "Yes, please."

Something flared in his gaze that she couldn't name, and Wolf grasped her hand and her purse in a show of possession that made her wetter. He led her away from the table, away from where Jerry gawped and sputtered. Liv was too stunned to even give him a parting piece of her mind.

They passed their original waitress near the entrance that led out to the hotel's lobby. "Give me a minute, Wolf?" Liv said, gesturing for her purse.

He halted immediately and passed her the bag.

Unzipping her wallet, she grabbed some bills and pressed them into the woman's hand. "I'm really, really sorry for the way he treated you. And that I didn't put a stop to it sooner."

The waitress shook her head. "Thank you, but I'm just glad you got away. That looked like the date from hell. We've all been in the back debating if we should rescue you."

"I've got that covered," Wolf said, his voice deep, gravelly, sexy.

The other woman grinned up at him. "I see that." She gave Liv an approving wink. "I hope your night gets better from here."

Glancing up at Wolf, Liv strongly suspected it would. Exactly what that might mean, however, she wasn't yet sure. "Yours, too," she said.

Wolf took her hand again and led her to a private nook in the hotel's lobby, shrouded in mood lighting and pulsing with the slow beat of a seductive, electronic song. For a long moment, he just stared at her, like he was debating, and then he stepped closer and got all up in her space. "I liked kissing you."

Liv released a shaky breath. "I liked it, too." Good God, what an understatement.

"I liked kissing you in public," he said.

She shuddered as if his words had been a physical caress. "I liked being kissed…in public."

"Did you now? Well then I wonder, sweet Olivia, what else you might like?"

In public. He hadn't said those words again, but she heard them anyway.

Tell him, Liv. See where it goes. What do you have to lose?

She felt a whole lot like she was standing on the edge of a cliff—a cliff she'd been peering over for a long, long time. She'd known for years that public displays of affection turned her on. She'd become aware forever ago that the idea of being caught, being *seen* having sex or being seduced was her favorite fantasy. She had plenty of experience with the fact that nothing got her off faster than imagining that fantasy, too.

But one thing held her back from jumping off that cliff with Wolf. Her ex's words still rang in her ear from the night she'd revealed her fantasies to the man she'd thought she could trust most in the world. And not just revealed them, but also asked him to make them come to life. Just once.

Geez, Liv. Fantasies are just that. I'm a partner. You're coming up for partner. If we got caught, it would ruin our reputations. And since when is normal sex not enough for you?

As if her wanting to try out a fantasy *wasn't* normal. As if *she* wasn't normal.

Three years had passed since they'd split, and Liv was ninety-five percent over that relationship. But Caleb's judgmental, dismissive tone about *this* still stuck with her.

"Where did you go just now?" Wolf asked.

"I'm sorry," she said, reflexively.

"Don't be," he said. "Just tell me what you want. You want to have a drink with me? I want that, too. You want dinner, because you didn't really touch yours? I'll get you that ribeye or anything else you want. You want me to kiss you again, I will. In a damn heartbeat."

Just tell me what you want.

It had been a long time since someone wanted nothing more than to please her. The fact that it was this beautiful man wanting to do so was more than a little heady.

"And what if…" Her heart hammered so hard her voice got breathy. "What if I wanted something more than kissing?"

* * * *

Wolf's big hands slid into Liv's hair, and he crowded her body with his until she was forced to tilt her head way back. "Then I'd take you up to my hotel room, press you against the window overlooking the street, and give it to you."

He braced for her reaction, and deep satisfaction roared through him when her eyes went wide, her mouth dropped open, and her breathing quickened. Thank *fuck* he'd read the signs right. The way she'd held her pose against that wall until he'd given her permission to move. The way she'd repeated his words back to him, just like he'd commanded. The way she'd melted into his kiss in the middle of the bar.

The way she'd answered his silent question, *Could you possibly want more than this, Olivia?* with a *Yes, please.*

This woman was submissive and she got off on being watched. Which meant she was perfect. Perfect for him.

Liv licked her lips, and her expressive eyes made it clear she was waging some kind of internal debate. But he was in no rush, because if he got her upstairs, he was going to take all damn night.

Finally, she nodded. "Yes, please," she whispered again.

"Say the words, Olivia. Tell me what you want." It'd been a long time since he'd played with someone not in the BDSM lifestyle, or at least exploring entering it, and so he wanted it all spelled out.

"T-take me to your hotel room. And...press me against the window."

He put his mouth to her ear. "And then what, sweetness?" Her floral scent was strong this close. He wanted to drink it down.

"And then...anything, Wolf. Everything."

Wolf had them in the elevator in an instant. He had her pressed against the doors the second they closed. And he had his tongue back in her mouth.

And, Jesus, where she'd been pliant before, now she was aggressive, kissing him back, pulling his hair, grinding against him. Giving him as good as she got.

They spilled into the hallway of the fourth floor. Breathing hard and nearly marching, he guided her down to his corner room, the one he'd reserved in case his interview with the submissive had led to a desire for something that required more privacy.

But never had he imagined *this*. The intensity. The connection. The raging lust.

Between choosing this bar of all the bars in Baltimore, the prospective canceling, and Liv wanting to be rescued—*and* being into what he was into, it was almost as if meeting Liv had been destined.

Wolf believed in signs. And when Liv stood up from that table, she'd given him one.

Maybe what he needed *wasn't* at Blasphemy after all. Maybe it was right here in front of him. In a fucking sexy five-foot-five-inch package, not including the three-inch heels with those seductive little ribbons.

The heavy door to the suite clicked shut behind them. Wolf held his ground as Liv ventured into the sitting room. She moved to the windows, exposed by the open curtains, and he knew exactly what she was seeing. The busy intersection below. Cars driving by on the street or idling at the stoplight. Throngs of people out for the game or heading to the rock concert at the venue a few blocks over.

He turned on one light, then another. It would soon be dark, and that light would draw attention from outside. Would make their window and any other illuminated window stand out in the darkness. Except their window would be filled with their silhouettes pressed to the glass, hot and sweaty and moving.

Should anyone look up and notice.

He came up behind her. His fingers brushed her hair aside and found the top of the zipper to her killer dress. He played with it, not yet pulling it down, not yet exposing her to his eyes—or all of theirs. "I want to fuck you against this window, Olivia. Do you want that?"

She went to turn, but he held her shoulders so that she remained looking outside. He could see her face well enough in the reflection of the glass, and he wanted her focused on being seen. "Yes, I want it," she said. "Though I've never done this before. Picking up a stranger. Um, the window..."

"We won't do anything you don't want to do, and I won't get upset if you change your mind. Now, five minutes from now, or five minutes after that. Do you understand?" he said, needing to be sure. Normally he'd talk to a submissive about safewords and boundaries and hard and soft limits, but that's not what this was. At least not yet. But that didn't mean he wasn't going to make sure she understood that she was in control. No matter what.

She released a breath. "Yes, thank you."

He shook his head and brushed his fingers back and forth along the neckline of her dress. "Don't thank me for that. You should never let someone have more of you than you want to give. And you should never expect less from someone than you'd consider basic courtesy."

"I think I need to get that on a T-shirt, Wolf," she said, chuffing out a small, nervous laugh. "It's good advice."

Wanting to reassure her, he kissed the skin below her ear. "Something else for that Monday to-do list."

Her laughter was real now. "I might need an assistant at this point."

Smiling, he kissed her shoulder, finding it hard to resist her. "Before anything happens, I want you to text a friend. Tell them where you are."

"Okay," she said. "You're...wow." She retrieved the phone from her purse and sent the text. "All done."

"Good," he said, setting her things aside. "I just want you to enjoy this, Liv." Smiling, he tugged at the zipper to her dress. It slid down. Slowly, so damn slowly. She gasped a little breath as the hotel's cool air hit the smooth skin of her back. "All you have to do is tell me to stop or slow down or do something differently, and I will," he said.

Liv nodded. "Don't stop." The dress fell to her feet in a flutter of material, exposing the long, curved slope of her back and the swell of her ass all wrapped in red lace lingerie.

God, she was brave and adventurous and so damn beautiful that Wolf could barely believe he'd found her. That he was going to have her. That she'd said *yes, please*.

He pressed his front against her back and let her feel the bulge of his hard cock against all her softness. "Hands on the glass, Liv," he murmured, lips to her ear.

With a little shiver, she complied. "I'm on the pill, but I want you to use a condom," she said.

"I was planning to, but I'm glad you said something," he said, smoothing his hands from her shoulders to her wrists and back again, then down her ribs, his fingers just skimming the sides of her breasts.

"God, Wolf," she said, another tremor wracking through her. Adrenaline, if he had to guess, which meant she was getting off on just the idea of this. Getting off on it, *hard*.

And her getting off hard was exactly what he intended to ensure. Because something inside him told him that, just like he'd said in the bar, he wasn't going to want to let her go.

Chapter 3

Liv couldn't believe this was happening, couldn't believe that she was about to let a total stranger fuck her against a hotel window. But she didn't want to be cautious or reasonable or respectable. She'd had a lifetime of that, and now she needed something more.

And if *not* doing this was normal, she didn't want to be that, either.

She wanted this. She wanted to know what it was like to *live* her fantasy. She wanted Wolf.

So as his big hands roamed her body, she gave over to having what she wanted. For once.

Running kisses over her neck, her shoulder, her back, he pushed the lace of her cheeky underwear over her hips and down her thighs. They dropped to her ankles.

"Step out of your clothes," Wolf said. "And spread your legs."

The command was so damn sexy, she felt close to orgasming from the words alone. She did what he told her to do, and then stood there in a red bra and a pair of heels. The reflection of herself looking like that would've been arousing on its own, but paired with Wolf's gaze meeting hers in the glass, they were a visual aphrodisiac.

"I want you to come before you take my cock, Olivia. I want you to come on my fingers with the whole world watching." His left hand pressed hers to the glass, while his right smoothed down over her belly and cupped her pussy.

A long moan poured out of her from the shock of the contact.

She'd had sex with two other men in the three years since she'd left her ex, but none of them had set her on fire the way Wolf was already doing.

And then his fingers spread her lips, glided through her wetness, slid inside her.

Her forehead sagged against the glass, her hair creating a little curtain around her face that at once left her feeling protected and exposed.

One finger, then two stroked her inside and out, penetrating deep, hitting her G-spot, circling her clit. He ground himself against her ass, and the feeling and the promise of his cock set her immediately on edge. On a groan, she turned her face toward him, and he rewarded her with a deep, wet, claiming kiss, his tongue mimicking in her mouth what his fingers did elsewhere. He tasted so good and he worked her even better, until she was panting and pressing and straining.

"Come on my fingers, Olivia. Come loud enough that the next room can hear you," he said.

And, Jesus, it was like his words had been lifted from her every fantasy. How did he know what she wanted to hear? What she needed to hear? What she'd always dreamed of hearing?

"Yes," she said. "Gonna come, Wolf." The sensation was climbing, tightening, spiraling.

His other hand moved to her chest and yanked her bra down, freeing her breasts so that they just touched the glass.

It was the extra exposure that did it.

She came on a scream. "Oh God, oh God, Wolf!" She slapped a hand against the glass. "Oh, my fucking God."

"Yes, Olivia. Yes," he growled, his fingers still moving, still filling her, still commanding her pleasure.

He kissed her one more time, and then he pulled away, leaving her panting and trembling. Even though his reflection revealed that he was undressing, she peered over her shoulder, wanting to see the real thing.

His chest was lean and broad, muscled but not ridged. His shoulders and biceps were works of masculine art, and she'd always had a thing for those parts of a man's body. His stomach was flat and...

She licked her lips as he pulled down his jeans. And oh man, his cock was freaking glorious. It jutted out from trimmed dark blond hair, long and curved upward, a bead of come at the tip. Because of her.

He retrieved a condom packet from his wallet, tore it open, and rolled it on. There was something about watching a man do that, particularly one she didn't know well, that felt so damn intimate. It was possibly a ridiculous thought, given that she was standing there mostly naked, but she still felt it. Because it meant that Wolf was about to be inside her.

And she couldn't wait another second.

"Please tell me we'll do this more than once," she said, her mouth running away from her. Her cheek suddenly felt hot against the cold glass.

He grinned. "Why's that?"

In for a penny, in for a pound, she guessed. "Because I can't decide if I want you more from the front or back, and I'm hoping maybe I won't have to choose."

Stroking his cock in that big fist, he nailed her with a scorching stare. "You want me, you got me." He stepped in close.

"Are you even real, Wolf?" she whispered, her head spinning.

"What do you think?" he asked, finding her entrance and sliding slowly, agonizingly, and finally deep.

"Yes. God, yes," she cried at the sensation of fullness.

"Keep your eyes on the streets, sweetness."

She exhaled on a long, tortured moan that made it hard to keep her eyes open at all. "That's so freaking good."

Tugging her hips back, he started to move. Long, smooth strokes that set her whole body on fire. That curve in his cock was pure magic, making his head drag against her G-spot on every single thrust. She dropped her face and breasts to the glass, her hair the only thing between her cheek and the cold surface.

"Damn, you're a fucking dream, Olivia." He gripped her hips harder, and the rhythmic smack of their skin sounded out in the room.

A horn honked on the street below.

Through the curtain of her hair, Olivia watched as people strolled on the sidewalk, crossed the crosswalk, and weaved motorcycles through the traffic. Three cabs waited to turn left, and a bus lumbered through the intersection. *How many of those people see us? How many of them just did a double take when they spotted us? How many of them might be taking a picture on their cell phone?*

All of that excited her. It was risky, of course. Especially now that she owned her own business. But that was why she'd turned her face to the side and let the length of her hair create a little barrier. They would see her breasts and her stomach and her legs. They might see a man moving behind her. They would *know* what they were seeing. But they wouldn't know it was her. Olivia Foster.

The riskiness got her off. Being seen got her off. Getting away with this got her off.

God, the reality was better than any imagining she'd ever done.

"I'm close again," she rasped, more than a little shocked. Because she'd never been able to come more than once with any other man.

"Good, because I want to feel that cunt clamp down on my dick, Olivia. I want to feel your come on my balls," he said, dirty words and hot breath equally thrilling in her ear. He flattened his palms against the front of her thighs and trapped her more fully against the glass. The change in position had him going deeper, the sensation more demanding, more intense. His thrusts shortened and quickened, forcing panting breaths out of her until she was deliciously dizzy.

The head of his cock created the most perfectly agonizing friction against that spot inside her. And that was what did it. "I'm coming, Wolf. Coming on you!"

"Christ," he bit out as her core squeezed him through five mind-blowing strokes. "You're so damn tight."

In the wake of her orgasm, he didn't let up one bit. He pushed both of her palms upward on the glass, his hands covering hers, and pressed her fully flat to the window.

"You still okay?" he rasped before dragging an open-mouthed kiss against the spot in front of her ear.

"Never better in my whole life," she managed with a breathy chuckle. She wasn't sure if she'd ever felt this alive before, and Wolf had been the one to make her feel this way.

"That's what I like to hear. You're going to make me come so fucking hard." His thrusts were short and hard and fast, his hips tilting as he ground deep. His breaths sounded like they scraped through clenched teeth. His hands and his body and his cock trapped her so that she couldn't move an inch. And she didn't want to. She wanted to be held there for everyone to see, against the window, getting the fuck of a lifetime. "Goddamn, Olivia," he growled. "God*damn*."

"Want to feel it," she said. "Want to feel it inside me."

He came on a shout, his hips moving roughly through the orgasm, his cock jerking into her with each spasm. Afterward, he exhaled against her shoulder. "You're amazing," he whispered.

And Liv was once again wondering if this man was truly real.

* * * *

Wolf got her the ribeye.

Room service had arrived a half hour before, and they'd devoured their picnic dinner sitting on the floor of the little living room, backs against the couch, the coffee table their dining table.

And, of course, Wolf made it even more interesting by demanding that she wear his green dress shirt—and only his dress shirt—when the waiter delivered the food. It *just* covered her ass. Even still, with their clothes in heaps all over the floor, it was perfectly clear what they'd been doing before the food arrived.

Her cheeks had heated at the man's purposeful efforts *not* to look, but she hadn't minded. Something inside her had liked that the man knew. And that Wolf had known that she'd like it.

As they ate, they'd had a million little getting-to-know-you conversations. His last name was Henrikson. He'd been born in Sweden but immigrated to the U.S. with his family when he was ten. He worked in IT and was a specialist in designing, installing, and monitoring high-end security systems. He co-owned that company with a friend. So he was a business owner, like herself. Somehow it seemed appropriate that he kept an eye on people for a living...

"Tell me more about your flower shop," Wolf said.

Liv smiled. "It's called Flowers in Bloom and it's been open for almost three years." She took a deep breath and let the next words fly. "It was the promise I kept to myself when I discovered my fiancé screwing another woman a month before our wedding." The revelation used to shame her, as if she'd done something wrong that had made him betray her, but she was over that now.

"Jesus, Liv, I'm sorry," Wolf said, his brow cranking down over suddenly stormy green eyes. There was always an intensity to his expression, but he could shift to fierce in a second.

"I'm not," she said, shaking her head. "Not anymore. Don't get me wrong, it hurt. But finding out that what I thought we had wasn't real was the best thing that ever happened to me. If I'd married him when he didn't really love me, my life would've been miserable. And I think I might never have left the law, which I was good at but kinda hated, to open my store, which is something I'm actually passionate about. Not only am I my own boss, but I get to help make people's lives beautiful with my flowers. Their weddings, their celebrations, their parties, their dinners. Even their funerals. I think, given the way this world is, we could all do more to create our own kind of beauty in it." She shrugged. "Probably sounds a little corny."

Shaking his head, Wolf tucked a strand of hair behind her ear. "Not at all. It sounds like someone's found her calling." He pressed his lips together and his gaze went distant. "It also sounds kinda familiar…"

Liv shifted her position against the couch and chuckled. "It does?"

His gaze ran over her face. Once, twice. "Did you used to have short hair?"

"Uh, yeah, I did," she said, surprised. "That was my boring-lawyer-hair phase. Wait, does that mean we've met?"

"Holy shit, we did," Wolf said. "At my friend and business partner's wedding. Do you remember Isaac and Willow Marten? Got married about two years ago."

The names rushed a slew of memories to the surface. What a sweet, fun couple Isaac and Willow had been. How amazing they'd looked on their wedding day, his white tux and her white gown, both with silver accents, so stunning against their warm, brown skin. Willow's wedding broom was only the second one Liv had ever decorated. She'd wrapped the handle with silver lace and beaded the handle jack and broom head with Swarovski crystals and tiny pearls, before finishing with a cascade of white roses and gardenias, each tipped with silver glitter. Willow had been so pleased that she'd invited Liv to stay so she could take pictures of her arrangements at the ceremony and the reception.

"Of course I remember that wedding," Liv said, staring at Wolf anew. And then recognition dawned. The groom had worn white, but the groomsmen had worn black, and Wolf had been among them. "We *did* meet! I don't know how I didn't recognize you sooner." Or, certainly, how she hadn't remembered his unusual name. Actually, she had an idea. Back then, Liv had still been so stung by Caleb's betrayal that she'd feared her interest in men had died with her engagement. Back then, weddings had still been difficult for her to do.

"Me, either," he said, smiling. "But damn. This is crazy that we ran into each other like this after meeting before."

"It is," she said with a grin. "And it makes me even happier that I caught Caleb. Because I wouldn't have met you then, and I also wouldn't be here with you now." Her pulse spiked at admitting how much being with Wolf pleased her, but she was thirty-one and had just let this man fuck her against a hotel window, so she saw no reason not to be honest. Putting herself out there was something she was trying to learn to do more of, every damn day.

Wolf leaned in and kissed her lingeringly. He tasted of red wine and buttery steak, a heady combination that had her moving in for more kisses when he tried to pull away. "I'm glad you're here with me, Liv."

His hand slid into her hair and he came over her, forcing her backward until they lay on the floor between the couch and the coffee table, Wolf's long, lean body covering hers. They kissed and writhed, hands wandering, clothes falling away again.

"I love how you submit to me," he whispered around the edge of a kiss.

Do you have any idea what your wedding night is going to be like?

The memory came from out of nowhere. A snippet of conversation between Willow and her bridesmaids from the room where the women had dressed for the ceremony. Liv had been unboxing their bouquets from the protective cartons in which she'd brought them. Laughing and teasing, the women had all stopped dressing to hear Willow's response.

Ladies, I'm a submissive, wife or not. If that man doesn't put me on my knees tonight, there's going to be trouble in paradise.

Liv still remembered how much her cheeks had flamed at the conversation that had followed. Because Willow and Isaac, and some of the other wedding attendees, it seemed, weren't just a little adventurous in the bedroom. They were all apparently into the BDSM lifestyle and belonged to a club where they could actually be open about that lifestyle with others who shared their interests. That such a place existed had been a revelation, but Caleb's words had still sounded out too loudly in Liv's head to allow her to do more than wonder about it then.

Even more than being a little embarrassed, though, Liv remembered how envious she'd been that Willow had found a man who knew what she wanted sexually—and gave it to her. Enthusiastically, unconditionally, and from the sounds of it, frequently.

Questions suddenly circled in Liv's mind. Questions about Wolf. At various points tonight, he'd commanded her. He'd made her *want* to please him. He'd read and anticipated her most private desires—and made them come to life…

"I want to be inside you again," Wolf said, blazing green eyes peering into hers.

"Yes," she said, unable to think when he looked at her that way. Like she was blowing his mind the way he was blowing hers.

He rose and helped her off the floor, and then he let his gaze do a long, lingering down and up over her naked breasts and bare pussy. "I'm a voyeur, Olivia. I get off on watching other people, and I get off on putting a lover in a situation where other people will watch her shatter because of what I do to her." He paused, letting those words hang there.

She swallowed hard, not shocked to learn this about him because that much seemed clear to her already. Instead, she was shocked because he put it out there so bluntly, so freely, so directly as if…as if it were perfectly normal.

And it was, wasn't it? *Damn you, Caleb.*

"I, uh, like that about you," she managed.

He chuckled. "I suspected you might. Because I think you're an exhibitionist."

"I…I am," she said, summoning the courage to admit this to someone again. *Say it. Tell him all of it. He won't judge you. You can trust him, Liv.* He'd proven that—with the text to her friend, with his encouraging words, with his promise to stop any time she wanted. "I *am* an exhibitionist. And I get off on being watched, on doing things where I might get caught, on the idea that other people might get aroused by watching me." The words spilled out of her in a nervous rush, but still, she'd said them, she'd admitted them.

"Good," he said, accepting her declaration unquestioningly. And damn if that easy, open acceptance didn't make something in her chest go tight and warm. "Then I have an idea that should please both of us."

She shivered at the promise of his words. "You lead, Wolf. And I'll be only too happy to follow."

Chapter 4

The rooftop pool deck was empty. At least for now. And that was perfect.

"It's beautiful up here," Liv said, walking past the closed-down bar and around the pool's edge, to the glass-and-metal railing that encircled the whole area. "City lights below and stars above."

All Wolf could see was Olivia, clad in a white towel tucked under her arms. Beneath, she wore only the red bra and panties he'd stripped from her before. A little coverage in case they ran into anyone on the way up. "Definitely beautiful," he said.

She turned, grinning almost shyly when she realized he was talking about her. "Can I tell you something?"

"Anything, sweetness." He came right up to her and braced his hands against the railing on either side of her. Two towels and her lingerie were all that separated them.

Lovely blue eyes peered up at him with emotions that played with things inside his chest in a way that was new. Powerful. Completely unexpected. He couldn't resist kissing her, tasting her, exploring her with his tongue.

At thirty-five, Wolf had been with his share of women. Working at Blasphemy gave him plenty of opportunities to find partners who shared his interests. But he'd never managed to go beyond playing to find a connection. Sometimes he wondered if that was because, at the club, it was all *so* easy, *so* available, *so*...almost predictable. He enjoyed the riskiness of exhibitionism and voyeurism, too. The thrill of it. The fear, and the overcoming of it. And those were harder to experience in a place where everything was so accepted.

Which was why he'd been wondering about remaining as one of the twelve Master Dominants there. Shouldn't he be more into the whole scene than he'd been lately? Once, it had meant everything to him, back when being one of the founding members had given him a community and a brotherhood and a safe place to be his truest self.

Things that Wolf could possibly introduce Olivia to...

Maybe that's why she intrigued him so much, called to him, made him *want*. In her eagerness and her uncertainty, she reminded him of the excitement he'd once felt. Made him want to feel that way again.

And he *did*, right here and now, with her.

Wolf pulled back from the kiss and loved the lust-drunk softness of her eyes. "What did you want to tell me?"

She licked her lips. "You're the first person who ever made me feel like it was okay. I mean, you know, the exhibitionism."

Satisfaction roared through him, curbed only when he studied her and found that uncertainty in her expression again. "It *is* okay, Olivia. Has someone made you feel otherwise?"

She gave a little shrug with one shoulder. "I told my ex. Asked him if we could try some things. He made me feel like I was being ridiculous and irresponsible. That it wasn't normal."

Anger clawed down Wolf's spine. That. That right there was the reason why he'd gotten involved with Blasphemy. He firmly believed that anything two consenting adults were into was not only okay and normal, but also absolutely no one else's business. Not everyone had that kind of tolerance and acceptance in their lives, though. He certainly hadn't. Blasphemy gave people a place to find it. And the fact that her asshole of an ex-fiancé had made her feel ashamed of her sexuality unleashed a fierce protectiveness inside Wolf toward her.

He wanted to tell her all that and more—and he would. But first he wanted to *show* her.

"I'm sorry he fed you that judgmental bullshit, Liv. You put yourself out there and he threw it in your face. What we did in my room... Did that feel abnormal to you?"

"God, no," she whispered. "I'd never felt more alive in my life. More...I don't know...myself."

Wolf nodded, the conviction in her words making him hard. He wanted her to feel all of that again. Because of him.

"Good," he said, tugging at her towel until it puddled at her feet. "Elbows on the railing."

Liv swallowed hard and her gaze cut to the right, toward the direction of the door from the elevator lobby. And then she complied.

"You sure?"

"Yes," she said. "Whatever you're going to do, I want it."

God, she was brave. And willing to be bold. It called to those same parts of himself. Nodding, he went to his knees. "Good, because what I want is your come in my mouth." As she gasped, he pressed kisses to her stomach, her hip bones, her thighs.

And then he pushed the red lace of her panties to the side and licked his tongue firm and flat over her clit.

"Oh, shit," she said, going up on her toes. "Oh, shit, that's so good."

Her praise drove him on, made him ravenous. He licked and licked, sucked and nipped. Gripping her ass in his hands, he canted her hips forward, allowing his tongue to venture deeper between her legs, to probe and plumb at her opening. She moaned and gasped and ground herself forward, sagging against the railing until he was half holding her up. He didn't mind one bit.

He sucked at her clit and flicked it fast with his tongue. Her thighs trembled. Her muscles strained. Her hand fell to the back of his head and held him down. All of which had his cock tenting the towel wrapped around his waist and him struggling to hold back from taking himself in hand.

"Wolf, Wolf, Wolf," she chanted.

He sucked her harder, willing her, forcing her, silently commanding her.

"Ooh, f-fuck," she rasped as her orgasm hit. He lapped up everything she gave him until her arousal coated his tongue and his chin. It was fucking glorious.

When she was steady again, Wolf rose to his feet. Making sure she was watching, he wiped at the wetness he wore with his hand, and then licked his fingers clean. "I could eat you all fucking night."

"Oh, my God," she whispered, a little tremor rocking through her. "Fuck me," she said, her gaze flickering toward the door again. "Please fuck me. I need you in me now."

He scooped her towel off the ground and led her to the furthest chair at the bar. He covered the metal lattice seat with the terrycloth and guided her panties off. "Sit. Now. Legs apart."

Damn, it was gratifying to watch her follow a command. Did she even realize how submissive she was? How much pleasure she received from being commanded and obeying? Wolf didn't think so, not when that close-minded asshole of an ex wouldn't consider ways of giving her even a little of the public sex she craved.

He glanced toward the door again, but couldn't see it from this last seat, angled as it was in the corner created by the curve in the bar top. Wolf suspected Liv would've gone along with sex standing right where they'd been, but he'd read enough partners' expressions and body language in his life to know that she was just the wrong side of concerned about being spotted over there.

He wanted her to be able to concentrate on pleasure. And nothing but. That was part of the reason why he'd had her send that text.

Removing the condom packet from where he'd tucked it beneath the towel at his waist, Wolf held out his arms. "Undress me."

Those blue eyes flared, and Liv couldn't hold back a little smile. "Gladly." She bared him, dropping the towel near his feet.

He rolled on the condom, then crowded in against the chair until his thighs hit the front of the seat. "Put my cock inside you."

Liv's mouth dropped into an oval. Grasping his length, she shifted forward and ran his head through the pink lips of her pussy. Finally, she lined them up and tilted her hips to take more of him inside.

Wolf's jaw clenched at the goodness of it. "Brace your hands on the seat and fuck yourself on me. Use me, Olivia."

Lighting him up inside, she did as he asked. Clutching the seat on both sides of her ass, she rocked her hips in a steady rhythm until she'd coated his length with her slickness.

"Fuck," he growled, watching her cunt swallow his cock again and again. "That looks so goddamned good."

"Are you...are you getting off watching me fuck you, Wolf?"

He nailed her with a stare, torn between wanting to reward and punish her for that taunting tone. Either way, he loved it. "How could I not? My cock was made for your cunt."

"Oh, Jesus," she rasped.

"Say it," he said. "Say that my cock was made for your cunt. Tell me."

She licked her lips. "Your cock was made for my c-cunt."

"Again," he said, the strain of letting her lead this pushing him to his breaking point. "Say it a-fucking-gain."

"Your cock was made for my cunt!" she nearly yelled.

"Better fucking believe it," he said, suddenly shifting to hunch himself around her. He hauled her ass just over the edge of the seat and leaned forward, using the leverage of the chair's back and a hand in her hair to hammer himself into her once, twice, balls fucking deep.

On the fifth hard stroke, she came on a scream, her pussy squeezing so hard she threatened to take him over the edge way before he was ready to fall.

"Come as often and as loud as you can," he rasped, using the position to grind against her clit on every thrust.

An airplane flew overhead. Car horns blared in the distance. The chair screeched against the concrete. But sweetest of all was the steady stream of moans and murmured declarations and ecstatic cries of *I'm coming, Wolf!* that spilled from Olivia's beautiful mouth. He wanted in there, too.

One hand still around the chair, he moved his other fingers to her mouth. "Suck me while I fuck you, Olivia."

Opening her mouth, she accepted two of his fingers. Sucking, licking, stroking with her lips and tongue. He nodded, loving the way it looked. The visuals were *everything* for him. And Olivia Foster was like a feast for his eyes. The pleasure and passion in her gaze. The way her full breasts bounced, splayed over the disheveled red lace, his cock penetrating her core.

He pushed his fingers a little deeper, testing her. One of her hands flew to his wrist, not to resist, but to anchor. And something about that little gesture shoved him hard toward release. "Take me as deep as you can, Liv. It looks so beautiful."

The backs of his fisted fingers bumped her lips, and her eyes watered as his fingertips touched the back of her throat. She gagged but held him there, her watering gaze on his.

Wolf flew apart. He came on a shout that made him more goddamned light-headed than he'd ever been before. Withdrawing his hand from her sweet mouth, he clutched her tight and drilled his cock deep, deep, deeper until she'd wrung him dry. And then he kept going because Olivia was suddenly clawing at his back and crying his name, another orgasm wracking through her at the hard frenzy of his own.

God, he didn't want this to end. The sex, this night, or his time with this woman.

Chapter 5

Wolf was still buried deep inside her, still nearly hard, and Liv was still panting when he lifted his gaze and nailed her with that brilliant green stare. "Spend the night with me here. I really don't want to let you go."

Butterflies spinning in her belly, Liv nodded. She didn't need to think about it. It was crazy how comfortable she felt with Wolf. How...connected, even. But maybe that's what it felt like when you finally found someone who accepted you for exactly who you were, kinky fantasies and all.

Of course, it didn't hurt that Wolf was seriously one of the hottest men she'd ever seen. That their conversation over dinner had come so easily, so naturally. That he understood her so fundamentally that he seemed to know she'd been uncertain about having sex against the railing. And that he was a freaking *fantastic* lover. With a magically curved cock. Couldn't forget that.

My cock was made for your cunt.

No way was she ever going to hear those particular c-words again and not remember this night, this sex, this man.

"That was amazing, Liv," he said, withdrawing from her. "*You're* amazing." He kissed her sweetly, slowly, appreciatively.

"If I am," she whispered, "you bring it out in me, Wolf."

"Sweet, sweet woman." He held out a hand and helped her down from the tall stool, and then he wrapped her in the towel again. "Care for a swim before we go down?"

Smiling, she ventured to the pool's edge and dipped her toes in. "Oh, my God, it's really cold."

"That's why you're supposed to just jump in," Wolf said, laughing. "Now you're thinking about it being cold."

"No, Wolf, seriously. Feel it." She gave him a challenging look.

Smirking, he moved toward the pool, then picked up speed and dove in over the six-foot marker, his lean body a work of masculine art. Liv's jaw dropped. He was going to regret that. Like, *seriously* regret it.

He came up on a shout. "Fucking hell."

Liv burst out laughing. "I told you."

He turned in the water, his expression like he was half in shock. "It's…it's not b-bad," he said, not selling it at all when his teeth clattered like that. "I grew up in the coastal town of K-Karlshamn and spent my summers swimming in the Baltic Sea. This is n-nothing."

She wasn't buying that for a second. "Uh huh. I think that's the first lie you've told me, Wolf Henrikson. And I'm not falling for it for a second." She backed up from the edge as he swam closer, because no way she was getting pulled in there.

He licked droplets from his lips. That man was sexy even when he was freezing to death. "Water's fine. I'm a s-stout Swedish man. I have ice in my blood."

She shook her head, still chuckling. "Yeah, well, I'm a skeptical American woman and I call bullshit." Man, she enjoyed him when they weren't having sex, too. He was playful and funny and so easy to be around.

Grasping the ladder, he reared up out of the pool, water cascading off of his naked body. Now there was a mental image she wasn't going to forget anytime soon. Except before she could replay it in her mind's eye, he shook out his short hair and stalked toward her. "Can I have a hug, Olivia?"

She backed up. "I don't think so. I'll take a rain check, though," she said, giggling again.

He moved faster. She weaved to put a table between them, though his cock being out in the open was super distracting to her agility.

"Just one hug, Liv. Is that so much to ask?" he said, smiling too.

Shaking her head, she pointed to ward him off. "You keep your icy Swedish hands off me until they warm up. I warned you."

He feinted right, so she went left, but then he bolted the other direction and caught her around the hips. She screamed and tugged, but he held fast, and then he molded himself to her. Ice. He was like ice.

"Fuuck, you're warm," he moaned. The grit in his voice would've been sexy as hell if his touch hadn't almost been painful.

"Aaaah! Get off me," she said, laughing and twisting and fighting. "You're a human Popsicle!"

"Keep grinding against me and I'll give you a Popsicle," he said, laughing.

"I don't like Popsicles!" she shout-laughed as she gave him a shove.

But he held tight. "You like *my* Popsicle," he said, guffawing.

Giggles devolving into super sexy snorting, she kept struggling. "How can you have a Popsicle after that water?"

"Because you're the hottest woman I've had the pleasure of meeting in longer than I can remember," he said.

Liv nearly gasped at the compliment, at the sentiment, at the sudden seriousness in the midst of their horseplay. When had any man made her feel so sexy, so brave, so wanted? She twisted to face him and cupped his face in her hands. "Jesus, Wolf. What's happening here?" she whispered. Because it felt like a lot more than what should be possible after just one evening.

He shook his head. "Something good, Liv. That's all I know for sure."

"Yeah," she managed, emotion thick in her throat. Definitely something good. And it was such a surprise to her. She'd thought she'd gotten over Caleb, and she had. Mostly. But she hadn't realized until tonight—maybe even until this moment—that he'd still held some sway over her. Because Wolf's interest in her, his acceptance of her, his desire for her all chased something away she hadn't even realized she'd still held onto—a little niggle of doubt about whether she'd ever find any of that after everything that'd happened with her ex.

Wolf shivered.

Liv chuckled, and the sound was all lightness amid the strong rush of affection she was feeling for him. "So, stout Swedish man. How about a hot shower before you die of hypothermia?"

He gave her a wink. "God, yes."

They showered together, an intimacy Liv hadn't shared with anyone in so long.

"You can have the water first," he said, backing her under the rain-style shower head as he kissed her.

"No, you first," she said. "You need warming up. Seriously, Wolf.

Your skin is still freezing."

"It's more important to me to take care of you," he said, tilting her head back and running his fingers through the length of her hair. Aw, man, this guy knew just what to say to make her melt. He reached for the shampoo. "Turn around." She did, and then he washed her hair for her. No man had ever done that before, and it felt so good she had to brace her hands against the shower wall in front of her to keep from swaying. "You're so damn sexy, Liv."

His voice roughened, but his hands kept strictly to washing her. Her hair, her body.

"Your turn now," she said. And damn, Wolf showering was something to see. He closed his eyes and tilted back his head. The water had turned his blond hair dark, and his position—hands at his reclined head—made all kinds of interesting muscles pop out and flex. "I wouldn't mind a camera right now," she mused, watching him.

His eyes popped open, and his cock stirred. "See something you like?"

She allowed herself a slow, lingering look. "Yes, sir, I do."

He was suddenly totally hard. "Jesus, Liv."

After that, he washed in a rush, toweled them both dry, and secured a towel around his hips again as she wrapped one under her arms, knotting it above her breasts. Then he guided her into the living room, where her dress still lay on the floor.

"Wolf, did I say something wrong—"

He whirled on her, his expression intense. "Olivia, get on your knees."

For a moment she gawped, her brain struggling to make sense of his behavior and his words. But everything inside her told her to just do it. *Kneel first, ask questions later.*

She knelt.

The tenting of his towel became more pronounced.

"Christ, you are…" He held out a hand to her. "Rise, please."

"Wolf, what is going on?"

"Would you come sit with me, Liv? There's something else I need to tell you."

* * * *

"No, you didn't do anything wrong," Wolf said, guiding them to sit on the couch. "In fact, you did something *so* right it's making me a little insane. So right for me." God, when the word *sir* had come out of her mouth, it'd been all he could do not to put her on her knees right that very second. And then he had, and she'd taken to the command without question or hesitation. "Olivia, I'm not just a voyeur, I'm also a Dominant."

"A sexual Dominant? Like, in BDSM?" she asked, her expression not as confused or as surprised as he expected.

"Yes, exactly."

"I wondered about that," she said. "I remember Willow and some of her bridesmaids talking about...stuff. And then when you reminded me that we'd met when you were one of Isaac's groomsmen, I wondered..."

He was going to need to send Isaac and Willow a fruit basket. Or offer to babysit their new little three-month-old. Because Liv's presence at their wedding was going to make this conversation go much better than it might've. A handful of times, Wolf had shared this about himself with women he'd met outside the lifestyle, and the reactions had run the full gamut. Repulsion. Disinterest or a feeling that it wasn't a fit. Or interest even though the woman wasn't truly submissive.

And true submissiveness couldn't be faked.

"How much do you know about dominance and submission, Liv?"

She gave a little shrug. "Not a lot, really. I mean, I've, er, watched some porn..." Her cheeks went pink at the admission.

"Come here," he said, putting his back into the corner of the couch and opening his legs to create a place for her to lay against him. "I need you closer."

Liv shifted so that her side was to his back, in his arms but still able to look him face to face. They smelled of the soap and the shampoo they'd shared, their bodies still warm from the shower. "Are you a member of their club, too?"

He chuckled. "The ladies were talkative that day, weren't they?"

Her expression dropped. "I'm not getting them in trouble, am I?"

"No, no. Not at all," he said, appreciating her protective instincts toward his friends. "I'm not just a member of the club, though. I'm one of Blasphemy's founders and owners. There are twelve Master Dominants who run it. Isaac, too. He and I joke that we're partners in both our day and night jobs. Each of us has areas of expertise on the operational side that we take turns managing. I work with Isaac on maintaining and overseeing the security systems and procedures."

"Okay," she said, suddenly frowning. "Wait. If you live in Baltimore, why did you have a hotel room?"

God, Wolf hoped this didn't make a difference to her, but she had a right to know. "Often, a Dom will meet prospective submissives in public places just to talk about their interests. Then, if things go well, they might come to some agreements about what they want and decide to do a scene. It doesn't always work that way. Sometimes, you just don't hit it off or you find your kinks or expectations aren't as well aligned as it seemed. Just in case the meeting does go well, I usually reserve a room, and I'd been stood up just before we met. In fact, I was getting ready to leave when I ran into you."

"Oh," she said.

Wolf studied her expression, a niggle of concern stirring in his gut. "Talk to me, Liv."

"I...I guess...that all makes sense."

"Damnit, I'm sorry if knowing I had other plans tonight makes you uncomfortable. I can only say that I truly believe this night went exactly as it was meant to be."

Liv shook her head. "Wolf, I was on a *date* when we met. I'm not upset that you'd had other plans, too. It just makes me realize how close we came to almost missing each other."

He kissed her because he felt the same way. "That would've been a tragedy, Liv."

She chuckled and nodded, running a finger down his bare chest, his abs, the semi-erect ridge of his cock beneath the towel. "Can you tell me more about what it means to be a Dominant?"

"First and foremost, it means that it's my responsibility to take care of my submissive in every way that she requires it. Her safety, her health, her pleasure. In a sexual scene, it's my job to read a submissive's body, her needs, her boundaries, and to create a connection through that scene that brings us both pleasure. It's more than just a role I play, though. It's an instinct, a need inside me, sexually and otherwise. It's just...who I am."

"That makes sense," she said. "And why did you tell me to get on my knees?"

Wolf just looked at her to see if she'd make the link herself. He really didn't think he had to spell it out.

"You think I'm a submissive?"

He rewarded her with a soft, deep kiss. "I think you *are* submissive. To know exactly what that means and what the expectations are within the lifestyle, though, would require training. But, yes, you're a natural."

"Even though I'm not shy or reserved?" she asked.

He rubbed his hand over her arm. "It's not about your personality, exactly. Strong men and women can be sexual submissives, Liv. One of my best friend's submissives is a former Marine. Submissives are often people who derive pleasure from obedience or being commanded. Or they derive pleasure from serving and pleasing another, or from being freed from decision making. For some, submissiveness is just what they need to achieve release. For others, it's not even about the sex so much as it is about being in service to another, in every way that might be required. Submission is a gift a submissive gives to a Dominant, and even though the Dom gives the commands, the sub can put a stop to it at any time. The submissive is in control because nothing happens without her or his consent."

"I see." Liv shifted on his lap, creating a gap in the towel between his legs. "You commanded me tonight, several times. And I... I liked it."

Wolf nodded, appreciating the methodical way she was approaching this, like she was taking apart what she knew and examining it from different angles. "You did."

"I-I've never had multiple orgasms during sex before," she said. "Is it awkward that I'm telling you this?"

He nearly groaned. "Not at all, Olivia. None of this works without open communication. That's why couples in the lifestyle often meet to talk about interests, limits, and expectations before anything sexual ever happens."

"Okay," she whispered. "Wow. This is...wow."

"Good wow or bad wow?" he asked, his gut clenching in case he was reading her wrong.

"Good wow," she said, with a little smile. "It's just...a lot to take in."

No doubt, and probably even more so when a lover had once made her feel bad about her sexual interests. "I'm not trying to push you into anything you don't want to do or explore, Liv. As you saw tonight, I don't have to be in full Dom mode to have sex or be dominant. But I also wanted you to know."

"I'm glad you told me, Wolf. And I'm definitely curious. I guess I sorta feel a little like Alice in Wonderland, except Wonderland was where I was always meant to be. I just didn't know how to get there. Or even if it was really real."

He nodded, appreciating the sentiment. "You're welcome down the rabbit hole with me any time, little Olivia."

She shifted again, and her voice came out husky. "You in full Dom mode must be…something."

He chuckled even as her words heated his blood. "If I were to put my fingers between your legs, would I find you wet?"

A shiver ran over her skin. "Yes," she finally answered.

That knowledge made him want to plant his face between her thighs again, but he wasn't getting distracted from this conversation until she'd asked every question she had. "What's turning you on, exactly?"

Pink filtered into her cheeks, and she ducked her chin. "Being close to you, for one."

He lifted her face with his fingers. "Look at me. I want you to see that there's nothing but acceptance here. Acceptance and interest, Liv. Okay?"

"Yes," she said, her eyes searching his. *Yes, Sir,* he heard. "Also, imagining what might go on in your club. All those eyes that might see what we do. And imagining how much more intense sex with you might be when you're in Dom mode."

"Would you like to find out the answers to those questions some time?" He nearly held his breath in anticipation of her answer.

"It's a little scary," she said. "But I think…yes. I would."

"Then you just name it. Any night you want. I'll take you to Blasphemy. And I'll introduce you to anything you want to explore."

Chapter 6

Liv applied the last touches to her makeup, her hands trembling just a little. Because she was going to a sex club tonight.

All week, she hadn't been able to stop thinking about what Friday night would bring.

Actually, that wasn't true. Half her thoughts were occupied by wondering about Friday night, the other half had been consumed with daydreaming about the incredible weekend she'd spent with Wolf.

Weekend. Not just night.

Neither of them had wanted to say good-bye on Saturday, so he'd extended his hotel reservation until Sunday, and they'd spent the time talking and walking around Baltimore's Inner Harbor and eating good food. Not to mention having more amazing sex. Against the window again. In the sauna at the gym. Against the door to the hotel room, so rough and loud there was no way people in the hall or other rooms hadn't heard.

Liv had loved every second of it. On some level, she'd feared that the seductive bubble in which they'd been secluded might burst once they were apart. But Wolf had allayed that concern by texting her throughout the week. Just to check in. Just to make her laugh. Just to tease.

And the result was that she'd been out of her mind with distractions and anticipation. So much so that, just this morning, she'd made an entire arrangement of red roses when the order was for pink.

She stepped into her heels just as the doorbell rang and spared herself one last glance in the mirror. Earlier in the week, she'd taken a picture of herself in a dress to make sure Wolf thought it was appropriate—because what did people wear to sex clubs???—and he'd told her that if she didn't wear it, he'd punish her.

Liv had no idea what that would entail exactly, but she'd worn the dress. A black vintage-inspired number with a formfitting cross halter top with a princess neckline, and a flared A-line skirt that ended just above the knees. She grasped her purse and rushed for the door.

And there Wolf was. Just as sexy as she remembered. Maybe sexier, standing as he was on the front porch of her townhouse wearing a pair of gray dress pants with shiny black shoes and a black button-down shirt. Rolled-up sleeves exposed his forearms.

"That picture did absolutely no justice to you in that dress, Liv," he said, drinking her in. He stepped right up to the threshold, took her face in his hand, and kissed her. A slow, exploring, lingering kiss, like he was tasting her, or sipping at her. It unleashed butterflies in her belly. "Hi," he said.

"Hi. And thank you." She grinned and suddenly felt on the verge of giddiness. For getting to see him again, for getting to go to Blasphemy, for getting to *be* with him again, whatever that might entail tonight. "Would you like to come in?" As he entered, she admired his ass in those pants. "Next time, though, I think you have to send me a picture of your outfit, too."

He arched a brow. "Why's that?"

She smirked. "So I can have a picture of…" She waved her hands at him. "…all *that* on *my* phone."

He chuckled and gave her a challenging look. "You can have any part of me on your phone that you want, Liv."

Her cheeks were hurting from smiling so much. "I'll keep that in mind."

"You do that," he said, surveying her living room. She tried to see it through his eyes. Large, framed Georgia O'Keeffe prints dominated her walls. *Petunias. Red Poppy. Jimson Weed.* The furniture was all neutrals, a cream-colored couch and chair and mission-style dark brown tables, to allow the flowers to stand out. A few framed photographs of family and friends filled one of the bookshelves. Once there had been more, but a lot of her friends had been Caleb's or law firm friends, and somehow, she'd lost or drifted apart from many of them when her relationship fell apart.

"Would you like the nickel tour?" she asked.

Wolf nodded. "I'd love to be able to picture you at home when we can't be together."

Gah! He took what could've been a simple *yes* and multiplied it by like a sexiness factor of at least a gabillion. At the back of the house, the kitchen and dining room were bright and airy, filled as they were with the rays of the setting sun.

She was just about to lead him to the staircase when she noticed him frowning at the vase of red roses on her table. Lest he get the wrong idea, she lightly rested her hands on his waist. "Today, I was so distracted that I made a client a bouquet of red roses when he'd ordered pink. I brought the mistake home to enjoy."

Those green eyes blazed at her. "Distracted, huh?"

"Very." She stepped in closer, until her breasts pressed against his chest. "Thinking about you is very distracting, Wolf."

His lips quirked in a crooked grin. "What if I said I liked you being distracted by me?"

Liv shrugged one shoulder and peered up at him. "Then I'd say keep doing what you're doing."

He licked his lips. "I think you'd better give me the rest of this tour before we never make it out of your house tonight."

Smiling, she led him upstairs. "Just my bedroom, a bathroom, and my office up here." She showed him the latter two before leading him into her bedroom. With her queen-sized bed, comfy reading chair, and two dressers, the room had never felt spacious. But now it seemed even smaller with Wolf there, eyeing her space like he was evaluating how and where he might take her. In point of fact, she was kinda looking around at the possibilities herself...

"You have a nice place, Liv. Comfortable and homey," he said.

"Thanks. I like it here. I can walk to the park and a coffee shop, and it's just a few bus stops to Flowers in Bloom."

He eased his big body to sit on the corner of the bed, then reached for her, bringing her to stand between his spread knees. "Do you have any questions before we go?"

She took a moment to think it through. He'd sent her information to read on Blasphemy, including the rules and membership information, which he informed Liv he'd be covering on her behalf; and on BDSM and submission, including instructions on safewords. He'd also sent her a list of activities for her to consider for her limits, which she'd checked off and stowed in her purse. "I'm sure I'll have a bunch of questions, but I feel like I won't know what most of them are until we're in the moment."

"Fair enough," he said.

"Can I still call you Wolf at Blasphemy?" she asked.

He pulled her to sit on his knee. "No. Please call me either Master Wolf or Sir. You should address all the Doms you meet this way. Sir is always safe if you're not sure."

Liv nodded, hoping she didn't mess up. Because there was a protocol to even speaking to Dominants or attached submissives that people observed. "I don't want to do anything to embarrass you."

"Not even possible, Olivia. I'll introduce you around, and everyone will understand that you're new and learning. And I won't leave you alone. Not even for a minute."

She smiled. "Okay, I'd appreciate it."

"Doing it as much for me as for you. If those roses made me temporarily insane, I can only imagine how I'd feel if another Dominant offered to play with you." He let the evidence of his possessiveness hang there until she was a little dizzy with it, and then he kissed her again. "Damn, sweetness, we gotta get out of here. Because I can't sit on your bed another second and not want to strip you down and bury myself deep."

"I'm not sure which you're trying to motivate me to want. Going or staying," Liv said with a little chuckle. She really adored how free Wolf was with his compliments, his praise, his desire for her.

"Tell me about it," he said. "But let's go. I want to show you off."

The words set her body on fire through the car ride across the city. Then they passed briefly through a public dance club called Club Diablo and spilled out into a private courtyard in front of an old church building. Liv spun around, taking in the nearly private oasis behind what appeared to have once been an old factory building. "No one would ever know this was here."

"The church was abandoned and in bad shape," Wolf said, squeezing her hand. "The city was going to tear it down. But my friends and I bought most of the block for both clubs. We thought this was perfect for the privacy our members want at Blasphemy."

"And it's beautiful," Liv said, looking up at the old steeple and the circular stained-glass window beneath it.

"Wait 'til you see it from the inside. The glass throws rainbows everywhere."

Inside, she gave Wolf—Master Wolf now—her checklist and stowed her purse in a locker, and then he led her out to a reception area where an intimidating-looking man sat behind the desk.

"Master Alex," Wolf said, greeting him. Which was when Liv noticed the black cuff around Wolf's wrist. Soft and worn. With an embroidered Gothic M. "I'd like to introduce you to Olivia Foster. She's my guest here tonight."

"Olivia," Master Alex said, standing. He had dark hair and darker eyes, almost piercing in their intensity. There was no denying the man was handsome, but there was something about him that, despite his politeness, was *too* intense for Liv. His gaze was hard to hold. "Welcome to Blasphemy."

"Thank you, S-Sir," she said, feeling a little self-conscious, like everyone would know she'd never done this before. She finally gave in to the urge to lower her gaze, and that's when she noticed that Master Alex wore a black cuff identical to Wolf's.

She sat and signed some paperwork while Wolf read over her checklist, and then Master Alex pulled out a drawer full of narrowed cuffs, a row of white and a row of red. He turned to Master Wolf, one eyebrow arched.

"Red," her Dom said.

Her Dom. The idea that he was hers, or could be hers, skittered tingles over her skin. "May I ask the difference? Sir?"

Wolf took the red leather into his hand. "White means unattached. Red means attached. I'd like you on your knees when I put it on your wrist."

Attached? He wanted her to wear something proclaiming her as his? She remembered what he'd said in her bedroom and how he'd looked upon seeing her roses, and part of her wasn't surprised. But it still spoke to a seriousness that made her feel like she could float.

"Now, Sir?" she whispered, half rising from the chair at the desk. She felt Master Alex's eyes on her, but she knew that she shouldn't look anywhere but at Master Wolf.

"Now, Olivia."

She sank directly from the chair to the floor, knees apart, like she'd read about, and eyes up on him.

"God, that's beautiful," Master Wolf said, seemingly comfortable saying such things in front of the other man. "Present your wrist, please. Right."

She held up her hand, and he fastened the red leather snugly around her skin. It was one of the most fascinating things she'd ever seen, because it made her feel claimed in a way she hadn't felt in so long. Possibly even ever. "Thank you, Sir," she managed.

He helped her rise and pressed a kiss to the soft spot above the cuff on the inside of her wrist. "You feel ready?"

"As ready as I can be. I'm a little nervous, but as long as we're together, I'll be fine," she said, being completely honest. Because she was excited, but she was also a bundle of nerves. About what she might see, about who she might see, about what might happen on the other side of the doors across the room, from which the bass beat of music was just audible.

"Count on it, sweetness," Master Wolf said.

"Olivia?" Master Alex said.

She peered at the other Dom, a cautionary awareness tingling down her spine. What was it about him that set her so on edge? "Yes, Sir?"

"Have a good night," he said. "It was nice to meet you."

"Thank you. You, too," she said.

Master Wolf shook the other man's hand, then led them through two sets of double doors until they finally entered the back of what was once the church. Olivia gasped. It was *gorgeous*.

At both ends of the vaulted ceiling, large circular stained-glass windows cast colors over the space—and the sun was setting. She could only imagine what the place would look like during the height of the day, when the side windows might be illuminated, too. Soaring frescoes covered the walls, and a large circular bar sat in the center of what had once been the nave. Leather couches and chairs sat here and there, some of them made private by arrangements of large-leafed tropical plants— palms, philodendrons, and bromeliads, to name a few. Against the beauty and elegance of the setting, the decadence of the music, people's costumes, and various sex acts happening where Liv could see or hear them, it was hard to know where to focus first.

She was at once enthralled by everyone's openness and a little shocked by it. Once, Caleb had made her feel ashamed for wanting to play out a fantasy with the man who was going to be her husband, and here was a whole club devoted to playing out fantasies—right out in the open where everyone could see.

"This is just the main floor of the club," Wolf said, pointing a few things out to her. The locker rooms, the public bathrooms, some dungeon furniture, a stage now used for demonstrations where the altar had been, a hallway down which private play rooms were located on multiple floors. In the middle of the space before the stage, a crowd of people danced under flashing lights to the pulsing, chanting, electric music.

"It's a little overwhelming," she admitted as he brought her to the bar. With the marble countertop and iron accents, it had an interesting vibe that was both modern and antique.

"I've got you, Olivia. I promise." He found a seat for her and raised his hand to the bartender.

The man headed their way, and he quite possibly had the best smile Olivia had ever seen. One that seemed a second from splitting into a grin or a laugh. One that might just as easily indicate he was up to no good. "Master Wolf," the man said gregariously. "How the hell are ya?"

"Master Quinton. I couldn't be better tonight. I'd like to introduce you to my Olivia." *My* Olivia! Liv didn't think she was imagining the pride—or the pleasure—in Wolf's voice.

"My, my, little Olivia. Welcome to Blasphemy. Where has my good friend been hiding *you*?" Master Quinton asked, holding out a hand that requested hers.

She looked to Wolf, and he gave her a nod, so she returned the shake. "Hi, Master Quinton. It's nice to meet you." He was a good-looking guy, but it was his humor and personality that created at least half of his charm, which was overflowing.

"Of course it's nice to meet me. I'm the awesomest. So awesome I'm sure Master Wolf hasn't been able to stop talking about me," he said, arching a brow.

She couldn't help but laugh. Where Master Alex set her on edge, Master Quinton put her right at ease and made her feel like an old friend, two things good bartenders often did quite naturally. "I'm very sorry to say, Sir, that Master Wolf has been otherwise indisposed."

Quinton barked out a laugh. "I like you, Olivia. You take care of this guy, okay? He's one of the good ones." He winked at Wolf and took their drink order, a whiskey for Wolf and a glass of champagne for Liv. The club had a two-drink-per-player maximum, but Liv didn't want more than the one. She wanted her senses about her tonight so she didn't miss a thing.

"Otherwise indisposed, indeed," Wolf said, giving her a smile. He led her to a couch partway between the bar and the dance floor, and guided her to sit between his legs as he had in their hotel room. Their position gave her a nearly three-sixty view of the club's main space—and the various activities in it. "Liking what you're seeing so far?" he whispered against her ear.

Liv nodded as she sipped at her champagne and tried to take it all in. A woman in spiked boots danced with a man wearing assless pants, and it was clear from the red handprints on the man's skin who was in control of that relationship. A man gave another man a blow job against the wall just past the dance floor. And a woman was tied spread-eagled to an X-shaped piece of furniture while two of the Master Doms— judging by the black cuffs they wore—tormented her with what looked like pleasure, given the woman's cries. "It's weird that I've had this hang-up when everyone here is so open."

Nodding, Master Wolf's gaze trailed to the threesome on the big X. "That's a St. Andrew's cross, and those are Master Jonathan and Master Cruz. They usually dominate a submissive together. How would you feel to be in that submissive's place?"

"With two Doms?" Liv asked, her gaze cutting back to the three of them. The blond-haired Dominant was on his knees, using his mouth and his hands between the woman's legs, while the dark-haired Dom smacked her breasts with a short instrument full of soft-looking black tails.

"Does that intrigue you?" Master Wolf asked.

"I…" She swallowed hard, her pulse picking up. "I wouldn't mind being her, being tied down and exposed to everyone. But two men seems a little…more than I'm ready for."

He turned her in his lap enough that they could see eye to eye. "It took me so long to find you, Olivia. I have no intention of sharing you." Relief flooded through her, and she nodded. "But I'm intrigued at this idea of tying you down and tormenting you while everyone watches. Maybe someday—" He pointed to the stage at the far end of the room. "—I'll get you up there and make a whole show out of you."

Liv's pulse spiked just imagining it. "Okay, Sir," was all she could manage to say.

Master Wolf laughed. "Don't worry. We'll work up to that."

She smiled. "Yes, please."

"Mmm. I remember the first time you said those words to me." Wolf pulled her to him for a kiss, forcing her to turn until she was straddling him on the couch. A million pairs of eyes landed on her back, watching them kiss, watching Wolf's hands run over her thighs and under her skirt. On a groan, he pulled away long enough to place their drinks on the end table. And then he was right back to her, penetrating her mouth with his tongue, dragging rough hands over her skin.

Knowing people were watching and hearing moans and cries of ecstasy from all around her, Liv was quickly needy and wet and a little dizzy with lust. And then Wolf's hands landed on her ass, rubbing and squeezing, his fingers digging in and making her wetter. "Wolf," she moaned.

Smack! His hand landed hard and unexpectedly against her left butt cheek. "How do you address me here?"

Oh God! "Master Wolf. I'm sorry," she said. The surprise of the spank unleashed twin reactions through her—a little humiliation and a whole lot of arousal. The latter confused her, even as she couldn't deny it. "I'm sorry, Sir."

His fingers curled into the waistband of her panties. "Rise and remove these. And bend at the waist when you drag them down your legs."

Liv's heart was suddenly a runaway train in her chest, racing fast and picking up steam. He helped her off his lap, and then she was standing in front of him. But not before she'd met the curious, interested gazes of a few of the onlookers around them. With a shiver, she met Wolf's gaze, too. His eyes were green fire.

It bolstered her. She bent over, reached under her skirt, and grasped the black silk-and-lace boy shorts. And then she slowly dragged them down her legs until she stepped out of them, one leg at a time.

He held out his hand, and she placed the panties into his palm. "Do you remember your safewords, Olivia?"

"Yes, Sir," she said.

"Use them if you need them." He arched a brow.

She nodded. "I will, but I don't need to, Sir."

"Good." The sternness on his face was so damn hot. "Then lift your skirt and turn around in a circle. I want to see what I'll be having tonight."

A shiver rocked through her, especially since she had a little surprise for him. Eyes on Wolf, she lifted the covering material up around her waist. If she thought she'd been wet before, it was nothing compared to how she felt now that she was standing in the middle of a room full of people showing off her bare ass and newly waxed pussy.

Wolf's eyes went wide. "Very nice, Olivia."

She turned in a circle, realizing that he'd made her do this so she'd see the audience that they were drawing. Her face and her body were equally on fire as she turned back to him.

He rose, made a big show of folding her panties and slipping them into his pocket, and then nodded. "You may drop your skirt."

Shakily, she let the material go, and felt torn between relief and regret.

He stepped in close. "That disappointed you, didn't it? Covering back up."

Relief or regret? Relief or regret? "A little, Sir," she was forced to admit.

"Hmm." He stepped back again, crossed his arms, tilted his head. Looked at her like he was evaluating. "That dress, it's all wrong, I think."

"What?" She looked down at herself, even more confused now. "You don't like it, Sir?"

"Too much, I think. I don't want anything to happen to it." Suddenly, he unbuttoned his own shirt. One button after another, with fast, furious flicks of his fingers. He whipped the black cotton off his shoulders, leaving him bare from the belt up. *God*, he looked freaking good. Cocky and confident, like a powerful businessman about to fuck his secretary on the conference room table in front of the entire board. Shirt in hand, his eyes narrowed. "Where did you go just now?"

"Here. I'm right here, Master Wolf," she said, her body's responses overwhelming. She'd never felt so aroused in her life, and it was almost too much to handle.

He shook his head. "Tell me. What were you just thinking about? I saw it on your face, Olivia. I want to know."

For just a second, she squeezed her eyes shut, and then she let the words spill. "It just...it just flashed into my mind when you took off your shirt. That you looked like…*oh God*…" She opened her eyes again.

"What?" he asked, nailing her with a hot, demanding stare.

"Like a powerful businessman about to have sex with his secretary on the conference room table in front of his board," she rushed out, face flaming.

His grin was slow and sly. "That's a hot fucking fantasy. I do love how your brain works, little Olivia." Without another word or any other preamble, he reached under her skirt and swiped his fingers between her legs.

She nearly screamed at the contact, so startled by it that she had to clutch at his biceps to steady herself.

He brought his hand between their faces. His fingers glistened with her arousal. Watching her watch him, he sucked the wetness into his mouth.

A little moan spilled unbidden from her throat.

"God, you're hot for this, aren't you?" he whispered.

"Yes, Sir."

"Just how far can I push you, Olivia?" he asked, his eyes searching hers. "Just how far are you willing to go?"

The question made her shiver again. As if her nervous system had been plugged into an electrical outlet, she couldn't seem to stop. Still, she knew she didn't want this night to end with her regretting that she hadn't been brave enough to go for something she wanted. And she wanted this. She wanted Wolf. She wanted him in full Dom mode, just like he'd said. "Push me hard, Master Wolf. I want anything you want."

His jaw ticked and his eyes flashed. "Brave girl," he said. "Take off everything except those heels. Right here. Right now."

Chapter 7

Wolf hadn't planned to push Olivia so hard so fast, but he also hadn't expected her to get so hot so fast. He suspected that if he'd left his hand between her legs for five more seconds, she could've come just from that little contact.

He fucking *loved* how turned on she was. Her breathing came fast. Her pulse jumped at her throat. Her eyes were dilated. And she couldn't stop shivering from the adrenaline he guessed absolutely flooded her system. She'd been so wet that she'd soaked his fingers from just one touch.

So he was going to push her, all right. Because he was suddenly ravenous to learn just how far he could take her, how far they could go *together*. He was flying because of how high *she* was flying, as if they were connected on a physiological level, as if her heart pulsed his blood. Damnit all to hell, but the connection they shared was blowing his mind. Because he hadn't been sure he'd ever find anything like it.

And then he met Liv.

On a shaky exhale, she reached for the zipper under her arm and undid the bodice of her dress. As she slipped out of the straps, he realized she wore no bra beneath it, which meant that disrobing immediately bared her beautiful, full breasts with their tightly erect nipples. Just like he'd requested before, she bent at the waist to push the dress down over her legs, and then she stepped out of the circle of material and rose again, clutching it to her front.

He shook his head and held out his hand. She gave him the dress. And then Wolf debated how he wanted to make her come.

"Too bad I don't have a boardroom table here," he said with a wink. Her cheeks flushed brilliantly, making him chuckle. "God, you're fucking beautiful."

She swallowed hard, and Wolf dropped her dress and his shirt to the couch, then went to her, drew her into his arms against him, and turned her so that his body mostly shielded hers. Now the crowd's eyes were on his back, but that meant that Olivia was forced to face everyone watching them.

"Wrap your arms around my shoulders," he said.

She hugged him, removing the last of the distance between their chests.

"Keep your eyes open while you come," he whispered, grinding his hard cock against her hip. He wanted her drunk with the pleasure that feeding her exhibitionist fantasies could provide. He wanted her to *see* exactly what they could be. Together.

"Sir?" she asked.

He cupped her pussy in his hand, pulling something close to a scream from her throat. "And say my name when you do," he growled, his fingers circling her clit.

The first orgasm hit almost immediately, and Olivia nearly shrieked, "Master Wolf!" as it made her shudder and moan.

"Again," he said, his movements alternating between firm circles against her clit and long strokes between her thighs that skimmed her opening.

"Oh God," she said, more of her weight hanging on his shoulders as her legs grew weak. "I'm going to…oh God." He pressed harder, faster. "M-Master Wolf, I'm c-coming," she nearly cried.

While her body still trembled, he kicked her stance wider. "*Again.*" He penetrated her pussy with his middle finger, using the heel of his hand to provide friction against her clit. She was soaking wet, slick and so damn tight. It was all he could do to avoid taking her to the couch and fucking her right there.

But it wasn't time. Not yet. He wanted to draw this out for her. He wanted to give her the whole fantasy. He wanted to let her experience that for which another man had made her feel ashamed.

So he let his fingers have what his cock badly wanted, masturbating her there in the club, his hand and her thighs wet with her come. "Christ, feel that pussy, Olivia."

Her hold tightened on his shoulders, her fingers digging in. "They're all watching," she rasped.

"Because your orgasms are fucking beautiful. Give them something else to see. Do it now," he said, finger fucking her hard, grinding his palm more firmly.

She thrust her hips to match the strokes of his hand. "Yes," she whined. "Yes, yes, yes."

The third orgasm stole her legs out from under her, and he caught her with an arm around her waist while she was still coming, while her pussy was still squeezing at his finger inside her. "Master Wolf," she chanted. "Master Wolf, Master Wolf."

"Jesus," he rasped, more turned on by her shattered surrender than he'd possibly ever been in his life. Scooping her into his arms, he cradled her against his body, and then he carried her to a more private grouping of seats on the far side of the room, away from the dance floor, tucked behind a wall that separated the old nave from a side hallway. He sat with her in his lap, his hand stroking her hair as the aftershocks of her orgasms continued to roll through her. "Just rest. I've got you."

It only took a few moments before one of the submissive waiters came to check on them. "A blanket, right away," Wolf ordered. "And when you have a chance after that, please retrieve our clothes from the couch behind the bar and bring us two bottles of water."

"Yes, Sir," the shirtless, shoeless young man said. He wore only a pair of Spandex short shorts and the white cuff that identified him as an unattached submissive. In less than a minute, he assisted Wolf in covering Olivia with a black fleece blanket. And within another five, he'd returned with the other requested items.

"I feel a little drunk," Olivia said when the man left them. Her bright turquoise eyes peered up at him, soft and sleepy. "I didn't think I had that much champagne…"

He smiled, adoring the way she was looking at him. "I think you're flirting with subspace, sweetness. Enjoy it."

"What's that?" she asked, the words a little slurred.

Subspace, for sure. "It's an intense, altered headspace some submissives achieve from the intensity of a BDSM scene or the intensity of release. It can feel like a lot of different things, from being sleepy to feeling drunk to almost becoming trancelike."

"Oh," she said with a breathy laugh. "I see. Master Wolf?"

"Yes?" He stroked the hair back off her face, loving being close to her, holding her, basking in the trust and affection plain in her expression. They'd only known each other for a week, but Wolf still felt a surprisingly strong connection to her, an unexpectedly deep desire for her. And not just sexually, though that was there in spades.

"When can we do that again?"

He burst out laughing, setting her off chuckling, too. "Eager, are we?"

"For that? Yes, Sir. Very eager, Sir." She grinned up at him. "Super. Eager."

"Greedy little submissive," he said, trying but failing to give her a stern look. He handed her some water and watched with satisfaction as she drank down half of the bottle. It made him want to feed her, to watch her eat from his hand, to sate her needs in another way. In *every* way. "What did you think of what we just did?" he asked after a moment.

Her gaze went distant. "It was…amazing. Overwhelming. A little scary at first, but then it was like, I don't know. I knew the people were there and that they were watching, but it became nearly impossible to concentrate on that. All I could feel was you and your hand and the way your words impacted my body. I never wanted it to stop but I also felt like I might die if it went on another second." She blinked. "Does that make any sense?"

"Total sense. I think you're articulating all this very well." And Wolf really appreciated that—that she could tell him with such specificity exactly what she was experiencing. It confirmed just how into this she was—and therefore just how right they were together.

More than that, the fundamental pleasure she got from this reminded him of how it all used to make him feel, too. Blasphemy was still new and risky and overwhelming to her, the people all strangers, and therefore, the stakes were high for her here even though it was a safe environment for her to play out these fantasies. And it not only reminded him of the edgy thrill he used to feel more of, it made him actually feel it again, too. And he cherished the hell out of that. He really did.

Being with Olivia Foster was giving him back something he'd been starting to fear he was losing. It was like getting a piece of *himself* back. And that played with things in his chest that hadn't stirred in a very long time. Maybe not ever.

And it was all because of the beautiful woman in his arms.

Right where he wanted her to stay. "Think you'd be up for dancing?" he asked.

"Like this?" she asked, her eyes going a little wide as she peered down at the blanket covering her nudity.

He chuckled. "Not naked, no. Though I don't dislike the idea, Olivia. Not one bit."

Smirking, she nodded. "I'd love to, then."

They rose, and she reached for her dress, but Wolf shook his head and pointed to the black cotton beside it. "Wear that."

"Y-yes, Sir," she said, slipping into his dress shirt. It was long enough that it just covered her ass in the back and the soft bareness of her pussy in the front.

"Just one button, I think," he said, securing the center one for her. "I meant to put this on you earlier, but then you distracted me with your dirty thoughts."

"I think you like my dirty thoughts," she said, a little shyly.

"I *know* I like your dirty thoughts." He winked, then he stood back and drank in the image of her like that. His shirt and a pair of high heels and the submissive cuff that proclaimed her as unavailable to anyone else but him. Damn. He wouldn't be forgetting *that* any time soon. "I love you in dresses, but I have to say, I'm a sucker for you wearing my shirts."

"I like it, too," she said softly.

"Do you now?" he asked, getting closer.

"Yes, Sir," she whispered.

"Those words from your lips make me so hard," he whispered back. Wolf pressed her palm over his pants against his hard cock.

She licked her lips and swallowed. "I like this even more."

"Jesus," he bit out, putting her hand in his. "Dance floor. Now."

They moved to the center of the large Friday-night crowd and swayed to a slower song, her loose breasts and hips brushing up against him so damn good. Then the music changed to a faster techno song with a grinding beat that was all sex set to music. She rubbed her ass against him. He made her ride his thigh as they swung their hips to the beat. Her shirt gaped open and drew up as she moved, earning them stares and appreciative glances that were setting Wolf's blood on fire.

Hers too, judging by the wetness he found when his fingers explored between her thighs.

Given how aroused he was, dancing with Liv was a beautiful torture. And it made his mind whirl with possible plans. He was going to fuck her tonight. The question was how and when and where.

He spun her so her back was to his bare chest again, and then he wrapped his arms tight around her front, molding her to him. Keeping them moving, he pressed his mouth to her ear. "I could fuck you right here in the middle of all these people. Just pull my hard cock out and sink deep."

"God, yes," she moaned, her head falling back to his shoulder. "Please, Master Wolf."

"I can almost feel it. How tightly your cunt would squeeze my dick, both of us standing up, our hips rolling and grinding. And then when I couldn't stand it anymore, I'd make you brace your hands against your knees, grab you by the hips, and hammer my cock into you so hard and fast you'd scream my name as all these people watched."

"I'm so close already," she whimpered. "So close, Sir."

"Yeah?"

She gave him a fast nod and pleading eyes.

He reached out and tapped on the shoulder of the Dom dancing immediately in front of Olivia. Wolf didn't know the man well, but that didn't matter. He just wanted an audience. Up close and personal. "Excuse me, but would you and your submissive be willing to watch my submissive orgasm?"

My submissive. Wolf fucking loved the way that sounded. He hoped she loved it, too. Even more, he hoped she might grow to want that with him.

The man looked at his little one and nodded. "It would be our pleasure."

Olivia moaned and a breath shuddered out of her.

"Thank you, Sir," Wolf said, and then he placed one hand on Olivia's throat and the other on her cunt, his fingers delving immediately and forcefully deep. "Don't come until I tell you to. And say *thank you* when it's over. Understand?"

"Yes, Sir," she nearly shouted as her fingers fisted in the sides of his pants.

He circled and stroked and tipped his middle finger inside her until she was babbling and begging and writhing against him. He didn't want her to fail, so he knew this couldn't last long, but he was going to draw it out as long as he could. For her.

"Don't come, Olivia. Not yet," he growled, their scene drawing more eyes as his hand worked her.

"Please, please, please, Sir," she whined, her hips rocking and straining.

He ripped her shirt open, popping the single secured button, and grabbed one breast in a tight hold. "Now. Come now."

Her body went taut and she held her breath for long seconds, and then she shuddered from head to toe, a high-pitched moan ripping out of her. "Thank you, thank you, thank you, M-Master..."

Flying high from the sheer intensity of her orgasm—and from how she'd just referred to him as if he were *her* Dominant and not just a Dominant—Wolf held her as her muscles went slack.

"Thank you for sharing something so beautiful with us," the other Dom said, a strain in his voice.

"Thank you, Sir," the man's sub said, her expression aroused, appreciative, envious.

"So good," Wolf rasped into Olivia's ear as he turned her into his chest. Despite the fast music, he swayed them gently, allowing her the time to get her legs back under her.

Her hands clutched at his shoulders as if he were her anchor. He wanted to be.

Goddamnit, but every minute he spent with her made that feeling stronger and stronger. Somehow, seven days ago, he'd been stood up and found his forever in one fell swoop.

* * * *

Liv could barely stand, barely think, barely breathe. And it was the best she'd felt in her whole life.

And it was all because of Wolf.

The man seemed to know her better than she knew herself. Because every time she thought, *I don't know if I can do this*, he proved that she could. And that she'd freaking love it.

He got her the way no one else ever had. Even Caleb, whom she'd been with for three years before they'd split. Which just went to show that time wasn't the only—or maybe even the best—indication of how well you knew someone. Or how well they knew you.

Her night with Wolf at Blasphemy had been amazing. The orgasms—obviously. But it was more than that. Wolf in full Dom mode was something to behold. The look in his eyes. The commanding tone of his voice. Even the way he held himself was slightly different— bolder, fiercer, taller. It spoke to something inside her, a voice she'd never before listened to, but that she now felt as if it'd always been calling out.

They'd danced for a long time after he made her come in front of that couple, until they were tired and sweaty and their voices grew hoarse from talking over the music. He'd introduced her to a few more people. Master Quinton's submissive, Cassia, who Liv hadn't had much chance to speak to because they were leaving to do a scene. Another Master named Griffin, and his submissive, Kenna, the former Marine that Wolf had mentioned. The four of them chatted for a while, long enough to learn that Kenna was assistant director of a veterans' outreach and advocacy association, and that she was interested in talking to Liv about providing the centerpieces for some of their events.

By the time they'd left, Liv couldn't wait to return. God, she really hoped they would. As Wolf drove his sleek Audi A8 away from the valet stand, he took her hand and held it against his thigh, giving her the courage to voice those wishes. "I really enjoyed myself, Master Wolf. I hope we can go again some time."

He brought their hands to his mouth and kissed her knuckles. "It's just Wolf now, Liv. And I'd like to take you there regularly, if you were interested. I'd like you to be mine."

The words unleashed a fluttery warmth in her chest that she hadn't felt in so long. But she knew what it was. Affection. Maybe even something more. *Probably* something more. "To be yours?" she asked.

"Yeah," he said, cutting a heated glance her way. "And not just at Blasphemy, either."

She squeezed his hand, not needing to think about it. Not with the way he was making her feel. There was something important happening here. Something big. Something good. Whatever it was, she wanted it. "Okay."

"Okay?" He arched a brow, green eyes flashing in the passing city lights.

"Yes. I'd like that, too."

"All right, then," he said, shifting his hips and making it clear he was aroused.

Which reminded her of the only thing she might've changed about the night—they hadn't had sex. And despite all the orgasms she'd had, she ached to feel Wolf inside her, for him to experience the same intense satisfaction that she had. Especially after what they'd just said to each other.

She leaned over and pressed her head to his shoulder. "Wolf?"

"Yeah, sweetness?"

She smiled at the term of endearment. "I want to make you come."

"Jesus," he said, shifting his hips again and chuckling. "You're killing me, Liv. I'm so fucking hard I can barely stand it."

She peered up at him, wanting to see the desire she heard reflected on that handsome, angled face. And it was. Oh, it was. She squeezed his cock through the pants, and the groan that spilled out of him was a heady thing. "I could suck you."

"Oh, Olivia, I will definitely be taking you up on that. But not tonight. Tonight, I'm going to be balls deep in your pussy. But we're both just going to have to be patient for a few more minutes." He removed her hand from where he throbbed but didn't let her go.

So, of course, now she burned with curiosity about what he might have up his sleeve. Was he going to take them back to her place and make her bed smell of hot Wolf and hotter sex? Because she wouldn't object to that at all. Or was he planning something else?

It only took another ten minutes before she found out.

Chapter 8

Patterson Park was just three blocks from Liv's house, a big green space in the middle of Baltimore, and one of the main reasons she'd bought a house where she did. Liv loved the park's community garden, its boat lake, the many events held there, and the beautiful Pagoda building that rose high enough that you could see down to the water and over to Fort McHenry from the top of it.

But Wolf didn't guide her to any of those locations. Instead, he took her to one of the pavilions filled with picnic tables and lit only dimly by the occasional path lights. Tension thick between them, neither of them spoke until the moment Wolf sat heavily on one of the benches in the middle of the pavilion, undid his pants and sheathed his cock, then pulled her to him.

"Fucking ride me, Olivia. Ride me so goddamn hard."

She was nearly trembling with need and adrenaline. She cast a glance at their surroundings, lifted her skirt over her still-bare ass, and centered herself over him. "Oh my God," she groaned as she impaled herself on his hard length.

His hands clamped down on her hips, holding her deep, forcing her to take all of him. Anyone who happened upon them would see a woman in a 1950s-style party dress sitting on a man's lap, never knowing she was stuffed full of his cock. But, *God*, Liv was just that. And it was so damn good.

"Move," he growled. "Fuck me."

"Yes," she moaned, bracing her hands on his knees as she lifted and lowered herself on his thick erection.

"Been dying for you all night," he rasped as they moved. "Been dying to make you mine."

Moaning, she kept up the deep ups and downs, her gaze scanning for witnesses, her mind half hoping to find them. Cars passed just a half block over and a couple's dark silhouette moved across a distant path. On such a nice night, all kinds of people were likely to be out, though the lateness of the hour would play in their favor.

Still, Liv could barely believe she was fucking someone in the middle of the park.

Or that she was so aroused that she was going to have to bite her lip to keep from screaming when she came. It didn't seem to matter that she'd come so many times earlier, because her body was winding up hard. From the risk of what they were doing. From the way Wolf's hands dug into her sides and hips and thighs through her dress. From the curses and dirty words spilling from his mouth.

"Christ, that pussy is so tight this way. I can't fucking get deep enough," he said, slamming her down and forcing a loud moan out of her.

Suddenly, he stood them up, bent her over the picnic table opposite them, and slapped a hand over her mouth. With his other hand, he flipped up her skirts, baring her ass to the night. And then he drilled her mercilessly hard and fast. All she could do was brace against the table and take what he gave her until she was screaming against his palm and he was groaning against her back, his hips jerking through each delicious spasm of his release.

"Fuck," he panted, dropping his forehead against her spine. "Jesus fuck."

His voice sounded wrecked, and it was the best thing she'd ever heard. She was so happy that tears suddenly sprung to her eyes and truths spilled out of her she hadn't even fully thought through. "This was the best night of my life, Wolf. Thank you."

"Aw, sweetness," he said, withdrawing from her and putting their clothes back together again. And then he drew her into his arms and held her close, his hand in her hair, his face pressed to hers. "Me, too, Liv. Something in you calls to something in me so strongly that you make me realize that my life hasn't been as complete as I thought. Not until now. I'm sorry if that's a lot to admit already, but—"

She shook her head. "It's not. Because I feel it, too." And so much more besides. All that emotion seemed like it should've been impossible already, but that didn't make the warm pressure in her chest any less present.

"I'm so damn glad," he said, tilting her head back for a sweet, tender kiss. "Let's get you home now."

"You could stay the night...if you want. I make a mean pancake," she said, her belly giving a little flip. Because he was right; despite the admissions they'd both made, this thing between them *was* moving fast. And she didn't want to overstep.

"I'd love nothing more than to fall asleep with you in my arms," he said, melting her heart. Then he grinned. "And to make your bed smell like me."

"Hmm. I was hoping you'd make the bed smell like *us*."

"Damn, Liv. You are perfect for me. You know that?"

She beamed at that, just a little bit. Perfect. It was the right word for how they seemed to fit together. That was amazing. But it was also kinda dizzying—how could she have found something this right, this true, this real...so fast? Could it truly be real? And could it truly last when three years with Caleb had ended in betrayal and humiliation?

"And pancakes would be amazing. Or I could take you to a restaurant and make you come underneath the tablecloth while the waiter watches," he deadpanned.

His voice chased the insecurities away, and Liv guffawed. "Well, that's an idea, too." They both laughed. And they were still laughing a half hour later when they crawled into her bed, her back spooned to his front, while he told story after story about funny things from his childhood, and that'd happened at Blasphemy, or that his friends had done. Just getting-to-know-you kinds of stories you told about your life and all the things that'd come before you met another person. Liv adored how much she enjoyed talking to Wolf, hearing about his life and his friends and his family, and how much they laughed, too.

She fell asleep mid-sentence, or maybe he did. Liv wasn't sure. Either way, she drifted off smiling with the knowledge that, despite their exhaustion, neither of them had wanted to give up on the magic of the day or the amazing connection they already shared.

* * * *

"Knock, knock," came a man's deep voice from behind him.

For maybe the tenth time, Wolf turned from the bank of computer monitors in Blasphemy's security control room to see who needed him for what. Tonight was one of their quarterly Blasphemous Friends nights, an open house of sorts where current members could invite pre-vetted prospectives for a special night exploring everything the club had to offer. Those who demanded strict privacy avoided these nights like the plague, but the events were a main way they expanded their membership base—and Blasphemy's operating income. And they required a shit-ton of advance work the day of the event to ensure they'd provided for every pleasure—and planned for every contingency.

But instead of some new problem walking through his door, Wolf found Isaac and Willow and a not-so-little baby boy in Willow's arms. "Three of my favorite people, right there," he said, rising from the chair.

He shook Isaac's hand and gave Willow a hug around the baby. Wolf had always thought her name was perfect, because she was tall and thin and so damn graceful she almost seemed to float. The two of them had met during a masquerade ball at the club three years ago, gotten married two years ago, and had this little bruiser here four months ago.

"Vaughn, my man, are you going to be Blasphemy's thirteenth Master?" Wolf asked, taking the chunky babe into his arms. "Because I bet you're already in charge at home." In response, the boy blew bubbles and Isaac laughed proudly.

"Pardon my saying so, Master Wolf," Willow said. "But bite your tongue. What is it with you Doms, trying to corrupt my sweet boy?"

Grinning, Wolf shrugged. "Sex on the brain?"

Isaac nodded. "Sounds about right."

"Well, Vaughn does *not* have sex on the brain," she said, crossing her light brown arms and giving both of the men in the room some serious stink eye.

"*Baby*," Isaac said to Willow. "You see how much he likes his penis. I'm just saying…"

Wolf busted out laughing. "It starts that early, huh?"

Willow rolled her eyes. "Apparently. Boys and their penises. If you don't cover the dang thing up quickly when you're changing him, you either get peed on or he manages to grab it in his little fist."

This time, Isaac and Wolf said it together, "Sounds about right."

"Oh, respectfully, Sirs, you two are hopeless. I'm going to go show him off to Master Quinton. He won't try to corrupt him."

Which set the men off laughing again. It was possible that Quinton was worse than any of them. In all the best possible ways.

Isaac dropped into a chair and scrubbed at his face. "What's new? You've been doing so much covering here and at our shop for me that I feel out of the loop."

"You've pulled plenty of weight, Isaac. Your priorities are right where they should be with your new family. Don't even give it a second thought," Wolf said, truly happy for everything his friend had found with Willow and Vaughn. Wolf himself should be so lucky, which of course had him thinking of Liv...

Nearly a month had passed since their first night at Blasphemy. And they'd been back at least once a week since. But they saw each other much more often than that, because for the past two weeks, they'd taken to spending many nights together at one of their houses. They'd have dinner and end up together. Or they'd stay up late watching a movie and fall asleep on the couch. Or they'd be so goddamned horny for each other that they just couldn't stand to part.

And, damn, the sex. The sex was a freaking revelation. And not just scenes at Blasphemy, either. The more Wolf exposed Olivia to, the more she wanted to try. They'd had sex in one of the bathrooms at Club Diablo, in the back of an otherwise empty matinee movie, on his sixth-floor apartment balcony overlooking a busy city street, and in her stock room during the workday. He'd fulfilled the threat of making her come at a restaurant more than once—with his fingers and with a remote-controlled bullet vibrator. And she'd blown him in a clothing store dressing room and in his car too many times to count.

Liv's excitement and enthusiasm made him feel alive again, making him realize just how much he'd been coasting these past few years. And he loved her for it.

He loved her.

Jesus, he really did.

"Wolf? Earth to Wolf." Isaac waved a big black hand in front of Wolf's face, then laughed when he blinked out of his thoughts. "What is *with* you?"

Unusual heat filtered into Wolf's cheeks, which of course Isaac noticed and ribbed him about. The fucker.

Chuckling, Wolf scratched his jaw. "I met someone."

Isaac's eyes went wide. "That's all I get? Spill, brother. Come on, now. Don't hold back on me."

So Wolf did. He laid it all out there. From the way they met, to the fast way they fell, to the fact that Wolf had been questioning whether Blasphemy was still right for him before Olivia helped him find himself again. "You've actually met her before," Wolf said, chuckling when Isaac frowned. "Liv Foster, owner of Flowers in Bloom. The florist at your wedding."

"No shit? Wait. I don't remember you hooking up with her there."

"We didn't. I didn't even recognize her at first. But it clicked that we'd met before when we finally got around to talking." He shrugged, his nonchalance masking just how damn special that night had been to him. The sex. The conversations. Hell, the whole weekend they'd spent together, and the connection it created. "But she's amazing, Isaac. Brave and sexy and smart and successful. This thing I've found with her, I think it's the real deal."

"Have you told her all that?" his friend asked.

"Some of it," Wolf said, his thoughts venturing where they'd been starting to venture more and more these past days. To questions of what came next... "But I haven't laid it all out there that directly. Yet. I'm starting to get a handle on exactly what I want with her, which I think could be everything. But we haven't been together that long. I don't want to make her feel rushed into anything, especially because she's been in a serious relationship before that went bad. Douchebag cheated on her a month before their wedding."

Isaac nodded. "Damn, that sucks. But it sounds like you know exactly what you want, Wolf. Given that, why wait? Who cares how long it's been if you feel like it's right?"

Wolf chuckled, appreciating the hell out of the sentiment and the straight talk. "Where the hell have you been again?"

"Neck deep in diapers, I kid you not," he said. "Wait 'til you have a baby. Because otherwise you'll never believe how much pee and poop something that little can generate. Hand to God."

The rest of the night alternated between speeding and dragging by. Wolf was busy as hell, working out processing glitches in prospective members' registrations, manning the cameras, and tracking the scrolling roster of players on the floor. Those with enough clout had scheduled interviews with some of the Masters, wanting a more personal introduction to the club before handing over their platinum credit cards for the most elite memberships, and Wolf had a couple of those on his schedule, too.

And all that was in addition to the fact that Olivia would be coming to the club herself sometime after ten o'clock, the final entry window for the event. Hopefully he'd get to spend time with her because he really didn't like the idea of her being alone out on the floor, but it all depended on how many fires arose that needed his particular brand of extinguisher. And she insisted that she could hang with Master Quinton at the bar or with some of the submissives with whom she'd begun to make friends.

All Wolf knew was that he was dying to see her. Because when the craziness of this night was over, he was taking Isaac's advice and laying it all on the line.

His feelings. His hopes. His wants.

Because Olivia Foster had finally taught him exactly what those were.

Chapter 9

Liv arrived at Blasphemy excited as ever, and maybe even more so than usual. Because the vibe tonight was electric, almost frenetic, from the collective excitement of all the new people experiencing the club for the very first time. Not that she was an old pro, by any means, but Liv still clearly remembered how she'd felt during her first visit here—that potent mix of anticipation and fear, arousal and adrenaline, surrender and flight.

And the club was packed.

A shiver ran over her skin. So many eyes…

Making her way through the press of the crowd, Liv finally managed to get close to the bar. But trying to find a seat there was a hopeless endeavor.

A hand fell on her arm. "Hey, Liv. Wanna join us?" It was Kenna, looking absolutely stunning in a silver-and-black sequined cocktail dress that matched the sleeve on her prosthetic arm. She'd lost everything below her right elbow while serving in Afghanistan, and Liv was so damn impressed by her that she already cherished her as a friend. "Some of the other subs and I claimed some couches in the hallway."

"That sounds great," Liv said, smiling at being included. After losing so many friends when she and Caleb fell apart, it felt really good to be making new ones again. New ones who knew the real her. "It's crazy in here."

"I know," Kenna said, leaning closer. "Cass and I were just saying we want our club back." They laughed.

"I don't know if I've belonged long enough to share in that sentiment, but I totally do."

Finally, they reached the grouping of couches located further down the same hallway where Master Wolf had cradled Liv in his lap that first night. *Some of the other subs* turned out to be about fifteen women and a few men, too. Liv didn't know them all. But she saw Kenna and Cass and Master Kyler's submissive, Mia, who ran an art gallery in town, all of whom she'd hung out with here a number of times.

And Liv also saw Willow, with whom she hadn't yet had a chance to reunite. "Willow!" Liv said, making her way through the tight-knit group. "It's so great to see you."

"You know, Isaac told me that you'd been brought over to the dark side in here. If I'd have known, I'd have happily made that happen two years ago," Willow said with a chuckle and a hug.

"Tell me about it. I wish *I'd* known what I wanted back then," Liv said, realizing how far she'd come in so little time. All thanks to Wolf offering to help a stranger caught up in the world's worst date.

Willow nodded, her soft curls a dark halo around her glowing, new-mother's face. "It's a process, trust me. Now that we have Vaughn, we're figuring out our relationship all over again."

"That sounds exciting and scary," Liv said.

"Little bit," Willow said. "But anything's possible when you're both in it together, you know?"

Liv appreciated that sentiment, especially because she felt like she had that kind of a relationship with Wolf. Or, at least, they were well on their way to building it. "And where is Vaughn tonight?"

"Believe it or not, he's asleep upstairs in the Masters' lounge." With a chuckle, Willow pointed at the coffee table where a baby monitor Liv hadn't noticed sat mixed in among the drink glasses and appetizer plates.

"Haha, training him early, are you?" Liv teased with a wink.

"Oh, my God, lady. You and Master Wolf must be a perfect match, because he said nearly the same damn thing."

Heat filled Liv's cheeks, but only because Willow was so right.

A warm body pressed to Olivia's back. "My, my, who have I found here?"

She smiled and turned in Master Wolf's arms. "There you are."

"I saw your name on the roster and then spotted you on the feed," he said, pointing up at the corner of the ceiling where a security camera perched.

"Mmm, were you watching me, Master Wolf?" she asked, heat stirring in her body from being in his arms again and from imagining him watching her when she didn't even know it. It made her want to perform for that camera. Undress for it. Orgasm in front of it. All knowing he was on the other side. His eyes on her every move.

"Always, Olivia. And this is giving me some interesting ideas," he said, eyebrows waggling.

She laughed. "All you have are interesting ideas, Sir. That doesn't tell me much."

He smirked and leaned in for a kiss. "I'll take that as a compliment," he murmured as his lips claimed hers.

"So do you have time to hang out or are you completely slammed?" she asked when they parted again.

"I have about fifteen minutes before I have to do an interview," he said.

"Fifteen minutes, huh?" She hoped her expression adequately feigned innocence as she peered up at him, even though her mind was all *Please have some dirty, dirty plans for those fifteen minutes!* "And what are you going to do with those fifteen minutes, Sir?" she teased.

He pressed his mouth to her ear. "Different crowd in here tonight. How adventurous are you feeling?"

Her belly did a flip-flop. He wasn't wrong, and that was both a little overwhelming and a lot intriguing. "I know you wouldn't push me to do something you didn't think I could handle, Sir."

"Mmm, you *are* feeling adventurous." His gaze ran over her dress— a white modern, mid-thigh number with sheer cutouts here and there that offered glimpses of her skin beneath. "And that dress is a fucking wet dream."

She grinned and did a spin, eager for him to see the cutout located almost dangerously low on her back.

His expression went all stern and intense, evidence that *full Dom mode* was now in effect. And she freaking loved when that happened.

Honestly, she loved every version of Wolf.

She just…loved *him*. Every time she admitted that to herself, it felt like her chest might burst open with the feeling.

"Come with me," he nearly growled as he took her hand and pulled her into the middle of the mayhem, to a padded wooden bench set up near the dance floor and the couch where they'd sat that first night. "Hands and knees on this bench right now. Head up, eyes forward. And don't move a muscle until I return."

Confusion and curiosity swamped Liv as she got into the position, but that was quickly washed away by the sea of eyes suddenly lighting up her skin with awareness. It was clear to everyone that something was happening, or about to happen, and so she drew a crowd even as Master Wolf melted away into it.

Thank God he told me not to move and how to hold myself, she thought, because otherwise she'd be hard pressed to resist the nervous energy flowing through her, not to mention the urge to duck her gaze.

Long—very long—minutes seemed to pass before Master Wolf finally returned. He got right in front of her face, something in his hand she couldn't quite make out when she knew she wasn't supposed to shift the position of her head or eyes. "You think you can tease me into taking you before I'm good and ready, little Olivia?"

Her mouth dropped open. "No, Sir. Of course not."

"Because that seemed exactly like what you were trying to do. Tease me into giving you the satisfaction you wanted right when you wanted it." He held up his hand. "And so I thought, if teasing is what interests you, I'd be happy to oblige."

Her heart tripped into a sprint, especially when murmurs and chuckles ran through the assembling crowd. It was a small dildo vibrator on two straps with a second vibrating piece those straps would hold tight to her clit.

Oh, God. He was going to torture her. For fun. In front of all these people. For…for *hours.*

"I'm sorry, Master Wolf," she rushed out, because she *was* sorry, and she was also hoping he might give her a reprieve. The last time he'd made her wear a bullet vibrator at a restaurant he'd been especially evil, turning it on every time the waiter stood at their table, forbidding her from orgasming until she was sweating and shaking and damn near to crying. And when he finally had allowed her to come, he'd made her do it so many times that he had to help her walk out of the place—*and* he'd had to walk behind her, because she'd soaked her dress.

And, yeah, Master Wolf had made sure the waiter had seen his fair share of it *all.*

Between that and the hundred-dollar tip her Dom had left, she imagined that waiter had a pretty damn good night. And that kinda got her off, too.

Damn Wolf. Maybe he knew her *too* well. Or at least it seemed so as he grinned and arched a brow. "I'm going to make sure all these eyes are on you tonight, Olivia. I sure know mine will be."

He moved behind her.

Rucked up her skirt. He'd instituted a no-panties rule for her club attire weeks ago, so his actions immediately bared her ass to the crowd.

Then he slid the straps over her heels and up her legs, forcing her to lift her knees one at a time as he went. Finally, he inserted the dildo, centered the butterfly-shaped flat vibrator over her clit, and secured the straps.

He smacked her ass for good measure, two good swats on each cheek, before putting her skirt back in place again.

He hadn't made a big show of it, and that almost made it worse—*more* humiliating—because he wasn't doing this for pleasure. This was his evil brand of voyeuristic punishment.

Liv was developing a love/hate relationship with it.

Oh, who was she kidding?

"Rise, assume the waiting position, and thank me," he said, voice stern and so damn sexy.

With as much grace as she could, Liv followed his command, coming to stand with her feet shoulder-width apart, her hands behind her back, her head up but her eyes down. "Thank you, Master Wolf."

He pressed a kiss to her cheek. "I'll see you in a little while, Olivia." He took one step back.

The vibrators turned on.

Both of them.

Strong.

The high-pitched gasping moan ripped out of her unbidden, and she nearly pitched forward from the sudden surprise of it.

A murmur of humor and appreciative approval rolled through the crowd, but she kept her gaze on her Dom. It was easy when he was so freaking hot in a pair of black dress pants and white dress shirt with the arms rolled up, and a silver vest. Her sexy businessman fantasy brought to life again.

But it was those green eyes that always sucked her in most.

Watching her, appreciating her, loving her. Did he feel it as strongly as she did?

"You're dismissed," he said, with a wink. "Go have fun."

* * * *

Thirty minutes later, Liv sought some privacy in one of the little nooks off the opposite hallway from where she and the other submissives had been hanging out. Because Master Wolf was making her insane.

She'd come twice in front of her friends—not to mention the strangers who'd been keeping an eye on her after her Dom's little show. Her friends understood. Hell, they even envied her, and she'd taken her fair share of teasing because of it. Liv was weathering it with as much good humor and chagrin as she could muster, because they'd *all* been there. And because she also knew that if she stood in front of one of the cameras and clearly mouthed the word *Red*, it would be over in a heartbeat.

Liv was in control.

But even with all that, she needed a moment to compose herself because he'd had the vibrator set at one of its higher settings for the past five minutes, and she couldn't decide if she wanted to cry or scream from the torment. What she did know was that her thighs were now wet from her orgasms, and the sensations twisting up tight in her body threatened that the next one might take her to her knees.

Finally, she found an unoccupied couch toward the front corner of the church and collapsed onto it. Closing her eyes, she could almost imagine that Wolf was there with her, whispering dirty little commands in her ears, using those big hands between her legs, that hard, curved cock pressed against her thigh, promising to make her feel so good.

She rolled her hips. His torture was going to make her come again. God. So close. She held her breath.

The vibrations stopped.

"No!" she cried to the empty room.

"So *this* was what you wanted? To be humiliated while everyone watched?"

Liv's eyes flew open, and her whole body went cold.

Caleb.

"What the hell are you doing here?" she asked, flying to her feet.

It'd been about a year since she'd last run into him, at a restaurant in the city. And he looked exactly the same. A few inches taller than her, brown hair and eyes, boy-next-door good-looking. But she never in a million years expected to see him *here*.

"I'm friends with one of the Masters. He thought I might be curious," he said, standing in the doorway to the little nook where she'd sought refuge.

Only to actually *be* humiliated by her ex-fiancé all over again. His words made her want to vomit and cry and run, but she wasn't letting him see any of that.

"You? Really?" She steeled her spine and crossed her arms, making sure her red cuff was visible.

He shrugged with one lazy shoulder as his gaze ran over her dress. And now she really did want to vomit. "I think about you sometimes."

She scoffed and headed for the doorway. "Gee, thanks. I *don't* think about you, Caleb. And I haven't in a long time. Now if you'll excuse me."

He stepped in front of her, blocking her way. "I watched what he did to you. I just can't believe that's how you want a man to treat you."

Shaking now, from anger and embarrassment and a whirl of emotions she couldn't even begin to name, Liv chuffed out a humorless laugh. "What I do is none of your business. Hasn't been for years. And why you'd think I'd care what *you* think about how a man should treat me after you'd been fucking another woman for months while we were planning our damn wedding, I can't begin to imagine!"

"Olivia," he said, grasping her arm.

She yanked away from him. "You don't get to touch me, Caleb. Now move out of my way."

"You used to want me to touch you. Maybe I just needed to do it how he does it. Maybe it would've been better between us then. I could turn you over my lap and spank you so hard. That what you like now?" He stalked toward her, and ice tingled down her spine.

"Don't touch me again," she yelled, glaring. "You twisted, pompous, close-minded *asshole!*"

Finally, someone heard them.

And not just any someone.

Master Alex. The most intimidating Master she'd yet met. She'd learned he was a sadist and that she was far from the only one who trembled in his presence. "Submissive, on your knees right this minute," he ordered.

Oh God. This was an order she did *not* want to obey. Not in front of Caleb. Not in a million years. But failing to disobey an order from any of the Blasphemy Masters was crossing-red-line territory for the club's submissives, and it would earn her discipline at Master Alex's hands and reflect poorly on Master Wolf, too. She was equally scared of both.

Liv knelt. Knees spread, back straight, hands on her thighs, head down.

"Jesus," Caleb muttered.

"What's the problem here?" Master Alex asked.

"I'm sorry, Alex," Caleb said. "We were just talking about playing together."

Her head whipped up. "We were *not.*"

Master Alex's dark eyes narrowed. "Talk out of turn again and I will take you over my knee."

Shaking with rage and bone-deep humiliation, Liv bowed her head. And got even madder when tears pooled in her eyes.

"I really did appreciate you inviting me, so I am sorry," Caleb continued. "I thought she was interested."

What the hell? Her mouth dropped open and words were out before she'd even thought to say them. "I can't believe you said that. That's a lie. I'm with someone else now!"

"Olivia!" Master Alex barked.

"But, Sir—"

"Caleb, please wait at the bar."

"Oh. Sure," he said. With one last glance at her, he was gone.

The first tear finally streaked down Olivia's face. And then another. She watched as Master Alex punched a text message into his cell phone, a deep scowl on his face.

God, he was so mad at her. This was bad. Really bad. And, Jesus, if Caleb was Master Alex's guest, of course he was going to take his side. And all she wanted was Master Wolf. Where was he?

After what felt like forever, Master Alex pocketed his phone and stood right in front of her. The hems on his worn blue jeans were frayed over a pair of black work boots.

"Look at me." She did. "Tell me what happened."

"He…he found me here. Made some unkind comments about my

choices and…interests. Then came on to me despite my telling him not to touch me and to let me leave. What he told you, none of that was true."

A storm rolled in over Master Alex's expression. "I'll handle him. But what am I to do with you?" Liv knew enough not to answer. "You spoke out of turn repeatedly. Didn't trust me to protect you. Did it never occur to you that I'd be able to tell that he was lying? How many times have I seen you and Master Wolf together? Besides which, you're wearing a red cuff. No other players should even be approaching you to do a scene."

Oh. He was right. More slow tears fell. What a mess this whole thing was. "I'm sorry, Master Alex."

He shook his head. "I know you are, but that might not be enough. I'll let Master Wolf decide."

"Decide what?" her Dom said, rushing into the room. "What the hell happened?"

Chapter 10

All Wolf knew was that his Olivia was crying, and he couldn't not touch her. He went right to her, a hand on her shoulder. "Liv, are you okay?"

"No," she said, more tears falling as her face crumpled. "Not okay."

Whatever Alex thought she had to be sorry for could wait. Wolf scooped her into his arms and carried her to the couch. He gave the other man a look he hoped communicated every bit of the anger coursing through him. Because some shit had clearly gone down and he was livid.

And at least some of that anger he directed at himself. Because he should've been with her. He should *know* what'd happened. Fucking open house night.

"I've got you now," he said, wiping her tears. God, she was so damn beautiful, and those tears were breaking his fucking heart. "And I'm sorry I wasn't here."

"I know," she whispered, visibly trying to pull herself together. "I'm sorry. I know this is probably embarrassing to you."

He cupped her face and kissed her, a firm press of lips to prove he was there, to make her *feel* it. "You could never embarrass me, Olivia. Don't ever say that again."

"A prospective member propositioned her," Master Alex said.

Oh, hell no. Beyond the possessiveness flooding his veins at the fact that this woman was *his*, Olivia wore a red cuff. And every person in the place—new or old-timer—had been made aware of the rules. Red cuffs equaled attached and therefore unapproachable for play by anyone but the submissive's Dominant. Period. "Has his ass been escorted out?

Because if not, I want to be the one to throw him the hell out the door."

Alex nodded. "I just notified Quinton to pull him off the floor, and then he'll have to be out-processed." He gave a troubled sigh. "I'm sorry to say this is partly my fault."

Wolf glared. "Explain, please."

"Caleb was my guest," Master Alex said. "I know him professionally. I never would've expected this behavior from him, and I'm sorry. I knew he was in the wrong the minute he started talking, but then Olivia disobeyed my orders to remain quiet so I could get to the bottom of the situation. That's what you heard us talking about."

"Caleb?" he bit out, then peered down at Olivia. In that instant, the name was too fucking unique for his liking. What were the chances?

She nodded, her eyes glassy again. "Yes, it was my ex. He...he saw us earlier. And then he found me here and..." She gave a helpless little shrug that shredded Wolf's insides. "...he said a bunch of stuff. Wanted to spank me and wouldn't let me by him to leave."

Christ. *Christ.*

He wanted to get up in Master Alex's face because the man had made a fucking colossal error in judgment that had put his submissive in jeopardy, but he wasn't letting her go to do it. Not while she was still trembling and teary, and definitely not when she thought her efforts to defend herself—whatever they were—might reflect badly on him. As far as Wolf was concerned, whatever she'd done had been all the way in bounds. "Master Alex, that man was Olivia's ex-fiancé, whose behavior was not honorable while they were together."

The other man blanched, which was impressive given how stoic he typically was. Master Alex was a total hardass, a closed-off wall of a man who rarely showed emotion and was damn hard to get to know. The submissives—men and women—who craved masochism worshipped him, but he wasn't one of the Masters with whom Wolf had gotten close over the years.

"Damn, Master Wolf. I'm sorry, to both of you."

Wolf nodded, all the acknowledgement he could muster just then. "I hope you'll understand I won't be punishing Olivia. Not for anything that happened here."

The other Dom held up his hands, his expression unreadable. "I'll leave it to you." He left.

Hugging her tight to his chest, Wolf pressed a kiss against her hair.

"I'm so fucking sorry, Olivia."

"Not your fault," she whispered. He held her for a long moment, just needing her in his arms, proof that she was okay. "Can you please remove this toy from me?"

"Oh, hell," he said. "Of course." He made quick work of it, setting the vibrator on the floor beside his feet. And then they sat knee to knee on the couch's edge, their foreheads leaning together, their hands entangled. "Are you okay?"

"Better," she said. "I was scared."

"Of what, sweetness?"

"Just…that I'd really messed up," she said, peeking up at him. "That I'd reflect badly on you. I know how important this club is to you—"

"Liv, please look at me," Wolf said, waiting to go on until she finally did. The tears had made her eyes startlingly blue, and he felt like he could fall into that gaze forever. "I need you to see that I don't think you messed up here. More than that, I need you to know. If it came down to you or this club, you'd be my priority, Olivia. I'd choose you. Every damn time."

She sucked in a breath, and her expression went so damn soft and sweet. "Master Wolf," she whispered. "I like playing with you here. The other Doms. Kenna and Cass and Mia. I feel like I have friends for the first time in a long time. A community. I adore that we share that. And that's saying nothing of the fact that this is a business for you, too. I don't want to make you choose."

He shook his head. "You're not, because you did nothing wrong. Your asshole ex did, and Alex did, and I did, but you did not. But I just wanted you to know."

She frowned. "You did nothing wrong, either."

"I should've been with you."

Liv squeezed his hand. "You can't be with me all the time. That's not how relationships work. Besides, I defended myself against Caleb just fine. If he'd have taken things one more step, I would've screamed my head off and brought half the club running."

Her words eased him and made him admire her so damn much. "My girl is always so brave."

"Your girl feels like kind of a mess," she said, and he loved hearing her call herself that.

She was his. And after all of this, he needed her to know.

"I'd wanted to do this differently," he said. "Make a moment of it. Make it romantic."

"Do what?" she asked, peering at him.

He took her face in his hand again, unable to stop touching her, holding her, being close. "Tell you that I've fallen in love with you. I love you, Liv."

Those turquoise eyes went wide and shimmery. "You…oh, my God, Wolf. I love you, too. I do. For weeks now. God, maybe even since the night at the park."

"Jesus," he rasped, pulling her into a tight hug. "I didn't want to make you feel rushed, but I've been feeling it, too. For so long. Damn, Liv, for me it might've been that very first night."

They laughed and kissed, soft, sweet, claiming presses of skin on skin.

"I want so much with you, Olivia. I just want to be in your life, and for you to be in mine, in every way."

Smiling so damn pretty, she nodded. "I want that, too, Wolf. I have never been happier in my whole life, and I'm so grateful you rescued me that night."

He chuckled. "Fate was looking out for us."

She grinned. "It totally was."

"Liv," he said, moving closer to her. "Would you consider moving in together? I want to go to bed with you and wake up with you and have meals with you and come home to you. You can move into my house, or I'll move into yours. Or, hell, we could look for a new—"

"Yes," she said, pushing him back against the couch and straddling him. "Yes to all of it. To any of it. I want to be the person you come home to, and I want you to be that person for me."

"Sweet, sweet woman," he whispered around the edge of a searing kiss that quickly flashed hot.

But he was done sharing Olivia with a million other eyes. At least for tonight. "Let's get out of here," he said.

"I'd like that."

He guided her through the club, taking a few of the security corridors back to registration to avoid the crowds.

"I have to grab my purse from the lockers," Liv said.

Wolf nodded. "Meet you right back here."

She'd barely left the room when the office door swung open and Master Quinton and Master Alex stepped out, deep-set scowls on their faces. A third man followed. Wolf didn't need to be told who it was.

The anger he'd restrained suddenly flashed through his blood, and he stalked toward them. "You Caleb?"

The guy's eyes went wide as he hung back at the door. Not so brave now, was he? "Yes, listen—"

"No, you listen—" Wolf ran into the wall of Quinton's chest as the other Dom blocked him from getting any closer. It didn't keep Wolf from trying as he jabbed a finger at the other man over Quinton's shoulder. "You don't come near Olivia. You don't talk to her. You don't get in touch with her. You see her on the street, and you turn around and go the other way. Understood? And if you say a word about anything that happened inside these walls tonight, this club will sue you for everything you have and then some."

"I'm a lawyer. I understand what an NDA is," he said, his tone laced with poutiness and fear.

"Time to go," Master Alex said, looming over Caleb as Alex escorted him to the door, then pushed it open. Crisp fall air spilled in. "I'll be seeking a new firm on Monday morning. That doesn't begin to reflect everything I'd like to do to your ass, but it's all, unfortunately, I can do. Security, see this man off the property."

Then the asshole was gone.

"Taking the trash out is my least favorite chore," Quinton said, a valiant but ultimately failed attempt at lightening the mood.

Wolf laced his hands on top of his head and unleashed a frustrated breath.

"Sirs?" came Olivia's quiet voice from the side of the room. "Is everything okay?"

"Aw, hell," Wolf said. "Come here, sweetness." The second she was at his side and in his arms, he felt better. "Everything's just fine."

"Is Caleb going to cause trouble for the club?" she asked, peering up at him.

But before Wolf could reassure her, Master Alex said, "He wouldn't *dare*. Between the three of us, we made sure of it. And I'm sorry for the whole damn mess, Olivia. I hope you can forgive me."

"I just heard you fire him for what he did here tonight," Liv said, wrapping an arm around Wolf's back. "That was pretty gratifying to watch. So please believe me when I say you are more than forgiven, Master Alex."

With a glint of appreciation in his dark eyes, the Dom gave a single nod and left.

"Champagne's on me next time, little Olivia," Master Quinton said with a wink as he made for the club again.

"Sorry, Sir, but as good as I'm sure that would be, I don't think Master Wolf or Cassia would approve," she deadpanned.

He blinked, then broke out into a guffaw. "Well played, subbie. I knew I liked you." He gave a wave and disappeared through the doors.

Here she was cracking jokes after the disaster of the past hour. There was only one thing Wolf could say about that. "I love you, Liv. So damn much."

"I love you, Master Wolf. Can we go home now?"

It was exactly what he wanted, too. So he took her home, spread her out in her bed, and gave her a glimpse of what their forever was going to be. All night long.

Epilogue

That night, Liv had told Wolf she'd never been happier, and that had been true. The amazing thing though? Each day of the month that passed after it, it was even more true than the day before.

She arrived at Wolf's office building and went up to the seventh-floor suite of M&H IT Security Services. She and Wolf had settled on a new place last week—deciding that both of their places were too small—and now they were painting and updating it before they moved in. And that meant they had a thousand decisions to make.

"Surprise, it's me," she said, knocking on Wolf's office door with a bag of take-out in one hand and a folder of paint samples and catalog inspirations in the other.

"Hey, Liv," he said, his face breaking out in a big smile. "Best surprise ever." He rose and emptied her hands, then took her into his arms for a lingering, playful kiss.

"Hopefully you'll still think that when I make your mind go numb trying to choose between atmospheric blue, vast sky blue, and bluebird feather."

He chuckled as they set out their Chinese food and sat side by side behind his desk. "Who knew there were this many shades of blue?" he said, using his chopsticks on a mouthful of lo mein.

"Wait 'til I show you the whites." She laughed as his eyes went wide and panicked.

As they ate, they settled on paint colors, furniture to order, and made a few calls to set up appointments for some of their other house-related chores. "I wish I could take care of some of this today," she said, "but I need to get back to the store soon. I want to try to finish the arrangements for Mia's gallery opening today so I can deliver them first thing in the morning." Between Kenna's association events, Mia's art shows, and Blasphemy's big masquerade costume ball coming up in just a few weeks, she'd gotten even busier at Flowers in Bloom. Busy enough that she'd hired some part-time help and might be able to bring on another person in the new year, too.

"We'll work through the list, don't you worry."

"I know," she said, cleaning up their lunch and finishing the rest of her water.

"Exactly how much longer do you have before you have to go?" Wolf asked, a look in his eyes that set off tingles in her belly.

She grinned and pressed the button on her phone to display the time. "Ten minutes. Maybe fifteen, tops."

A slow, evil smile grew on his face. "Plenty of time for what I have in mind."

She arched a brow. "And that is?"

Without another word, he took her hand, guided her down the hallway past his and Isaac's team working in open-concept cubicles, and through another door, which he closed behind him. Then he drew the vertical blinds to the interior windows, blocking out the hall beyond. Mostly.

"I can't have a meeting in here without thinking of your fantasy. And wanting to bring it to life." He nodded to the big conference table behind her.

Liv's body immediately heated. "Now? But your employees—"

"Which is why you'll need to be quiet and I'll need to be quick. Hands on the table, Olivia."

"Holy shit," she whispered, but she totally did what he said. Because who was she kidding? Just thinking about doing this, and that someone could walk in at any second, had her wet.

He roughly pulled down her jeans, but left them hanging at her thighs. And then he was behind her, parting the fly to his jeans and bumping her ass with his fist as he rolled on a condom.

"Hold on tight, sweetness, because this is going to be hard and fast." He filled her in one punctuated thrust.

She slapped her own hand over her mouth and went face down to the table.

"That's it," he whispered. "That's fucking it."

While she hung on to the edge of the cool wood, Wolf hammered at her with fast, hard, rough strokes that had her wanting to scream at how good it was. Instead, she pressed her hand tighter to hold the threatening sounds in and imagined a half dozen men in sharp suits filling the chairs around them. Watching. Nodding. Maybe even wanting a turn.

"Oh, already, Liv?" he asked on a dark, hushed chuckle. "You're squeezing my cock so damn tight."

A whine spilled from her throat.

"Quiet," he bit out. "They'll hear you. They'll come and see your cunt filled with my dick, Liv. Jesus, it looks so good, too."

He grabbed her hips, yanked them out from the table, and absolutely drilled her.

She came on a smothered scream, her body shaking and thrashing against the wood.

Wolf was right behind her, jerking and shuddering until he collapsed down on her back.

And then the only sound in the room was their panting and the rush of her own pounding blood past her ears.

"God, Wolf," she whispered, absolutely shattered in the best possible way. "I have to lay here forever now. I can't move."

"Oh, sweetness, I think that can be arranged," he said, kissing her cheek.

They chuckled and dressed quickly, and then Wolf was guiding her back down the hall again, past the friendly faces of his colleagues, most of whom she'd at least said hello to before on previous visits.

Did they know? Had they heard? And would Wolf ever stop making her feel so damn alive?

She didn't think so, and it was the best feeling ever.

He handed her the folder of materials and her purse, then walked with her to the elevator. "Have a good day, Liv. See ya tonight." He kissed her softly.

She loved knowing he'd be coming home to her. "You, too, Wolf. I love you." She stepped into the elevator.

"Love you more," he said, with a wink.

And she couldn't stop smiling the whole rest of the day.

* * * *

Also from 1001 Dark Nights and Laura Kaye, discover Hard As Steel and Hard To Serve.

Sign up for the 1001 Dark Nights Newsletter
and be entered to win a Tiffany Key necklace.

There's a contest every month!

Go to www.1001DarkNights.com to subscribe.

As a bonus, all subscribers will receive a free
1001 Dark Nights story
The First Night
by Lexi Blake & M.J. Rose

Discover 1001 Dark Nights Collection Four

For more information go to www.1001DarkNights.com.

BLADE by Alexandra Ivy/Laura Wright
A Bayou Heat Novella

DRAGON BURN by Donna Grant
A Dark Kings Novella

TRIPPED OUT by Lorelei James
A Blacktop Cowboys® Novella

STUD FINDER by Lauren Blakely

MIDNIGHT UNLEASHED by Lara Adrian
A Midnight Breed Novella

HALLOW BE THE HAUNT by Heather Graham
A Krewe of Hunters Novella

DIRTY FILTHY FIX by Laurelin Paige
A Fixed Novella

THE BED MATE by Kendall Ryan
A Room Mate Novella

NIGHT GAMES by CD Reiss
A Games Novella

NO RESERVATIONS by Kristen Proby
A Fusion Novella

DAWN OF SURRENDER by Liliana Hart
A MacKenzie Family Novella

Discover 1001 Dark Nights Collection One

For more information go to www.1001DarkNights.com.

FOREVER WICKED by Shayla Black
CRIMSON TWILIGHT by Heather Graham
CAPTURED IN SURRENDER by Liliana Hart
SILENT BITE: A SCANGUARDS WEDDING by Tina Folsom
DUNGEON GAMES by Lexi Blake
AZAGOTH by Larissa Ione
NEED YOU NOW by Lisa Renee Jones
SHOW ME, BABY by Cherise Sinclair
ROPED IN by Lorelei James
TEMPTED BY MIDNIGHT by Lara Adrian
THE FLAME by Christopher Rice
CARESS OF DARKNESS by Julie Kenner

Also from 1001 Dark Nights

TAME ME by J. Kenner

Discover 1001 Dark Nights Collection Two

For more information go to www.1001DarkNights.com.

WICKED WOLF by Carrie Ann Ryan
WHEN IRISH EYES ARE HAUNTING by Heather Graham
EASY WITH YOU by Kristen Proby
MASTER OF FREEDOM by Cherise Sinclair
CARESS OF PLEASURE by Julie Kenner
ADORED by Lexi Blake
HADES by Larissa Ione
RAVAGED by Elisabeth Naughton
DREAM OF YOU by Jennifer L. Armentrout
STRIPPED DOWN by Lorelei James
RAGE/KILLIAN by Alexandra Ivy/Laura Wright
DRAGON KING by Donna Grant
PURE WICKED by Shayla Black
HARD AS STEEL by Laura Kaye
STROKE OF MIDNIGHT by Lara Adrian
ALL HALLOWS EVE by Heather Graham
KISS THE FLAME by Christopher Rice
DARING HER LOVE by Melissa Foster
TEASED by Rebecca Zanetti
THE PROMISE OF SURRENDER by Liliana Hart

Also from 1001 Dark Nights

THE SURRENDER GATE By Christopher Rice
SERVICING THE TARGET By Cherise Sinclair

Discover 1001 Dark Nights Collection Three

For more information go to www.1001DarkNights.com.

HIDDEN INK by Carrie Ann Ryan
BLOOD ON THE BAYOU by Heather Graham
SEARCHING FOR MINE by Jennifer Probst
DANCE OF DESIRE by Christopher Rice
ROUGH RHYTHM by Tessa Bailey
DEVOTED by Lexi Blake
Z by Larissa Ione
FALLING UNDER YOU by Laurelin Paige
EASY FOR KEEPS by Kristen Proby
UNCHAINED by Elisabeth Naughton
HARD TO SERVE by Laura Kaye
DRAGON FEVER by Donna Grant
KAYDEN/SIMON by Alexandra Ivy/Laura Wright
STRUNG UP by Lorelei James
MIDNIGHT UNTAMED by Lara Adrian
TRICKED by Rebecca Zanetti
DIRTY WICKED by Shayla Black
THE ONLY ONE by Lauren Blakely
SWEET SURRENDER by Liliana Hart

About Laura Kaye

Laura is the New York Times and USA Today bestselling author of over thirty books in contemporary and erotic romance and romantic suspense, including the Blasphemy, Hard Ink, and Raven Riders series. Growing up, Laura's large extended family believed in the supernatural, and family lore involving angels, ghosts, and evil-eye curses cemented in Laura a life-long fascination with storytelling and all things paranormal. Laura also writes historical fiction as the NYT bestselling author, Laura Kamoie. She lives in Maryland with her husband and two daughters, and appreciates her view of the Chesapeake Bay every day.

Learn more at www.LauraKayeAuthor.com

Join Laura's Newsletter for Exclusives & Giveaways!

Discover More Laura Kaye

Hard As Steel
A Hard Ink/Raven Riders Crossover

After identifying her employer's dangerous enemies, Jessica Jakes takes refuge at the compound of the Raven Riders Motorcycle Club. Fellow Hard Ink tattooist and Raven leader Ike Young promises to keep Jess safe for as long as it takes, which would be perfect if his close, personal, round-the-clock protection didn't make it so hard to hide just how much she wants him--and always has.

Ike Young loved and lost a woman in trouble once before. The last thing he needs is alone time with the sexiest and feistiest woman he's ever known, one he's purposely kept at a distance for years. Now, Ike's not sure he can keep his hands or his heart to himself--or that he even wants to anymore. And that means he has to do whatever it takes to hold on to Jess forever.

* * * *

Hard To Serve
A Hard Ink Novella

To protect and serve is all Detective Kyler Vance ever wanted to do, so when Internal Affairs investigates him as part of the new police commissioner's bid to oust corruption, everything is on the line. Which makes meeting a smart, gorgeous submissive at an exclusive play club the perfect distraction…

The director of the city's hottest art gallery, Mia Breslin's career is golden. Now if only she could find a man to dominate her nights and set her body—and her heart—on fire. When a scorching scene with a hard-bodied, brooding Dom at Blasphemy promises just that, Mia is lured to serve Kyler again and again.

Then, as their relationship burns hotter, Kyler learns that he's been dominating the daughter of the hard-ass boss who has it in for him. Now Kyler must choose between life-long duty and forbidden desire before Mia finds another who's not so hard to serve.

About the Blasphemy Series

12 Masters. Infinite fantasies…
Welcome to Blasphemy

Books in Series

HARD TO SERVE
BOUND TO SUBMIT
MASTERING HER SENSES
EYES ON YOU
THEIRS TO TAKE (Coming September 2017)
ON HIS KNEES (Coming early 2018)

Theirs to Take

A Special Crossover Release with Jennifer Probst's Reveal Me, *A New Book in Her Steel Brothers Series*

Two Hot Fantasies. One Night at Blasphemy. Coming September 19, 2017.

She's the fantasy they've always wanted to share...

After serving in the navy, best friends Jonathan Allen and Cruz Ramos become partners in their sailboat building and restoration business and at Blasphemy, their BDSM club. They share almost everything—including the desire to dominate a woman together.

All Hartley Farren has in the world is the charter sailing business she inherited from her beloved father. So when a storm damages her boat, she throws herself on the mercy of business acquaintances to do the repairs—stat. She never expected to find herself desiring the sexy, hard-bodied builders, but being around Jonathan and Cruz reminds Hartley of how much she longs for connection. If only she could decide which man she wants to pursue more...

As their friendship with Hartley grows, Jonathan and Cruz agree that they've finally found the woman they've been looking for. Her reactions make it clear that she's submissive and attracted to them both. But as they introduce her to their erotic world, will she submit to being theirs to take...forever?

Mastering Her Senses
Blasphemy Book 2
By Laura Kaye

He wants to dominate her senses—and her heart...

Quinton Ross has always been a thrill-seeker—so it's no surprise that he's drawn to extremes in the bedroom and at his BDSM club, Blasphemy, where he creates sense-depriving scenarios that blow submissives' minds. Now if he could just find one who needs the rush as much as him...

Cassia Locke hasn't played at Blasphemy since a caving accident left her with a paralyzing fear of the dark. Ready to fight, she knows just who to ask for help—the hard-bodied, funny-as-hell Dom she'd always crushed on—and once stood up.

Quinton is shocked and a little leery to see Cassia, but he can't pass up the chance to dominate the alluring little sub this time. Introducing her to sensory deprivation becomes his new favorite obsession, and watching her fight fear is its own thrill. But when doubt threatens to send her running again, Quinton must find a way to master her senses—and her heart.

* * * *

The quip on Quinton's tongue died when a flashing red light under the bar's edge caught his eye. An emergency in one of the rooms. He glanced at the tag over the light to determine which one, then slammed the drinks down in front of his friends harder than he'd intended. "Shit, G, sorry. Emergency in the dark room. Get someone to cover?" he said, moving without waiting for an answer. He knew Griffin would have his back.

Quinton moved as fast as he could without calling undue attention. Their members knew that the Masters and a team of other Doms who worked as monitors responded to all sorts of problems around the club, some as mundane as an equipment malfunction and others more delicate situations involving disputes between players in a scene. Hell, a few months ago, Quinton had responded when Kenna broke down during a bondage scene, and Griffin had called for help extricating her from his intricate ropework. Sex at the extremes was bound to run into a few issues, which was why consent and safety were hallmarks of BDSM and Blasphemy itself. But none of that meant any of them wished to distract players from their pleasures with worry or curiosity, either.

Off the main floor, Quinton picked up his pace as he moved down the long hallway off of which most of the themed play rooms were located. The dark room was at the far end. Master Wolf came up beside him. "Hey, man," he said.

Quinton gave him a nod. "Didn't know you were on tonight, Wolf. Good to see you."

A little taller than Quinton, the guy had dark blond hair, the brightest green eyes you'd ever seen, and a chiseled Scandinavian face that turned heads all over the club. "Running the security control room. Relieving Isaac because the baby's sick," he said, referring to Isaac Marten, their head of security operations, who had a two-month-old son.

"Damn. Sorry to hear that," Quinton said as they closed in on their destination. The dark room was actually a series of three interconnected rooms. In the center was a pitch-black bedroom, accessed only through two changing/waiting rooms on either side of it—one of which let out into this hallway, and the other of which let out into a different hallway so that the players couldn't run into each other before or after the anonymous scene. The dark room was very popular, and given Quinton's interest in sensory deprivation, it was one he'd used many times.

He heard someone in distress before they even got inside.

Quinton and Wolf burst through the door to find one of the monitors trying to calm a woman curled on the floor, gasping like she couldn't breathe. She wore a slinky bronze dress that bared most of her legs.

"What happened?" Quinton asked, grabbing a blanket from a shelf and going to his knees beside her. He tucked the soft fleece around her.

"I don't know," the monitor said. I sounded the alarm but she told me not to call an ambulance when I asked.

"She just freaked out. I swear. Nothing hardly happened between us," a shirtless man said from the doorway to the dark bedroom.

Quinton hadn't even noticed him there, but Wolf was already questioning him. He nodded to the monitor, a Dom in his forties, and then peered up at Master Wolf. "You all clear out. Debrief him and get his information."

"You got it, Q," Wolf said, motioning the other men out into the hall. "Call if you need help."

As they left, Quinton brushed the woman's shoulder-length hair back off her splotchy face. "We need to get your breathing under control or I have to call an ambulance."

"No…no…I…it's…" Clenching her eyes, she shook her head and growled as if in frustration.

Damnit, he needed to do something for her. The part of him that needed to care and soothe decided, and he scooped her off the floor and carried her to the couch. Everywhere they touched, her pulse hammered against her skin. If this was a panic attack, it was one of the worst he'd ever seen.

He sat with her in his lap, the blanket still wrapped around her, and cradled her so that they were facing each other. "Breathe with me, little one. Do you hear me? Look at me and breathe with me." Striking hazel eyes with flecks of gold cut to his. Almost familiar…

Focusing, he exaggerated one breath, than another, and another, until she struggled to match her rhythm to his.

Griffin appeared in the doorway, questions clear on his face. Quinton spared him the smallest of glances and gave a single shake of his head. Griffin nodded and closed the door. Quinton had this. The others would be there in a heartbeat if he was wrong, but he didn't think he was.

Because the woman's body was calming. Her breathing was evening out. Her pulse was slowing. Her muscles were losing their tension.

"That's it. That's good. Just watch me and breathe with me. Don't stop. We'll kick this thing, don't you worry." He stroked his hand over her hair, wanting to soothe her. The color was so rich it almost matched the bronze of her dress. Her hair was beautiful and soft. As was the rest of her, all golden skin and pretty curves. Her weight felt good in his arms. She turned her face into his hand, just the littlest bit, and he stroked her hair again. A jagged scar ran along her forehead and into her hairline over one eye.

The scar triggered the oddest thought: *That wasn't there before.*

His gaze cut back to those eyes. Hazel with the gold. And he suddenly knew he'd seen them before. Years ago. Right here at

Blasphemy. A name clicked into place.

"Cassia?" he asked. Cassia. As in Cassia Locke, a submissive he'd flirted with quite a few times and was once supposed to play with…but she'd stood him up the night of their scene.

"Y-yes, Sir," she whispered. "H-hi, Mas-ter Q-quinton."

So she recognized him, too. Did she remember that night? He shook off the thought. Their history wasn't something to deal with just then.

"Hi yourself, kid." He gently scratched his fingertips against her scalp and concentrated on taking slow, deep breaths that she mimicked. Studying her, Quinton noticed another scar on her right shoulder. Her hair was also much longer than the almost boyish style she used to wear. Finally, Cassia went limp in his lap, and her ease unleashed a satisfaction in his blood. "Feeling better?"

She gave a long sigh, the sound exhausted and defeated. "As better as I can feel after utterly humiliating myself. Sir."

He shook his head. "No such thing happened. Not as far as I'm concerned."

Her gaze skittered away.

"Did I tell you to stop looking at me?"

Cassia's eyes snapped back to meet his. "No, Sir."

Her obedience unleashed even more of that satisfaction. The attraction of BDSM, to him, was as much about the psychology of it as the physicality of the acts. Her reaction—that obedience—represented an ingrained instinct, a need to serve, a desire to surrender. And that fucking heated his blood. He arched a brow and nodded. "Good girl."

She shifted in his lap, but kept her eyes on his. The movement reminded his body that he'd been planning to find a partner, but he locked that shit down tight. First, because she'd been through something tonight he didn't entirely understand. And second, because given that she'd stood him up and never bothered to follow up to explain, he wasn't sure what to make of her anyway. And trust was kind of a thing, for him. Well, for most Doms, really. Which meant he needed to know.

"Now, tell me what happened," he said, nailing her with a stare. "And tell me the truth."

On behalf of 1001 Dark Nights,

Liz Berry and M.J. Rose would like to thank ~

Steve Berry
Doug Scofield
Kim Guidroz
Jillian Stein
InkSlinger PR
Dan Slater
Asha Hossain
Chris Graham
Pamela Jamison
Fedora Chen
Kasi Alexander
Jessica Johns
Dylan Stockton
Richard Blake
BookTrib After Dark
and Simon Lipskar

CPSIA information can be obtained
at www.ICGtesting.com
Printed in the USA
LVHW032358191121
703873LV00004B/88